Also by John Ling

People Pie: Juicy Portraits in Poetry

MRS LOUD
&
MRS QUIET

Mrs Loud and Mrs Quiet

Published by The Conrad Press Ltd. in the United Kingdom 2023

Tel: +44(0)1227 472 874
www.theconradpress.com
info@theconradpress.com

ISBN 978-1-915494-64-1

Copyright © John Ling, 2023

The moral right of John Ling to be identified as author of this work has been asserted in accordance with the Copyright, Designs and Patents Act 1988.

All rights reserved.

Printed and bound in Great Britain by Clays Ltd, Elcograf S.p.A

Typesetting and cover design by The Book Typesetters
www.thebooktypesetters.com

The Conrad Press logo was designed by Maria Priestley.

MRS LOUD
&
MRS QUIET

AND OTHER WACKY STORIES

JOHN LING

Contents

Mrs Loud and Mrs Quiet	9
Takeaway	24
Breaking it gently	43
Tools in the van	57
Stuey's night out	70
The witch and the gardener	79
Leave me alone.	95
The diva of St. Dunstan's	113
Danny's dish	123
Carnival	133
Blackbird diplomacy	140
A tale of two dogs	149
The last sunrise	164
Aftermath	170
Zoe the wrestler	186
Zoe's revenge	196

Mrs Loud and Mrs Quiet

'Muuuum!'

Joseph had crept into his mum's bedroom again at one a.m, having been woken by the noises from next door.

'What love?' Mary mumbled from beneath her quilt.

'They're doin' it again, Mum.'

'Oh dear,' she sighed. All right love, bring your quilt in here and lie down on the floor.'

Mary groaned, and buried her head in the quilt again, snuggling up to her partner's broad back. She too could hear the sounds from next door, even two rooms away, and she knew what they meant.

At breakfast next morning Joseph was lethargic and yawning over his Rice Krispies. It was the same every weekend, and he did not want to go to school on the Monday.

'Do I have to go, Mum?' He tried it on every time.

'Yes, you do, love, you know you do. We can't make excuses every week just 'cos you're tired. What we gonna tell the teacher, eh?'

What she really meant was, what could *I* tell the teacher?

My neighbours were at it again late last night.

Richard, her partner was packing his bag for work, listening to this conversation for the umpteenth time.

'Listen Joseph, I'm tired as well every Monday morning, but I can't go moaning to my boss saying I couldn't sleep last night, can I. I'd get the sack, lad. It's summat we all have to learn if we want money to live on.'

He just about squeezed past the neighbour's partner's car which was partly blocking Mary's driveway. Looking back, he muttered something offensive, as he noticed their curtains were still closed at eight on a Monday morning. ''S'all right for some!' he groaned.

Mary was smoothing down Joseph's hair and straightening his collar as he tried to wriggle out of her way. 'Anyway, a man's coming tonight to talk about it. So, keep your fingers crossed.'

'What FOR?' Joseph blurted.

'Just to talk about it, love.'

'You said council man came before, and nothing changed.'

'Yeah, well this is not a council man. He's called a mediator. I don't know what he does, but he says he might be able to help. Now you get off or you'll be late love.'

*

George knocked on the front door at six o'clock. It was promptly opened by Mary, who was quite smartly dressed for a Monday evening.

'Mrs Brown? I'm George from mediation.'

'Yes, come in love.'

'Shall I take me shoes off?'

'No, you're all right,' she said, although she would rather he did, because of her cream coloured fluffy carpet. 'Sit you down on the sofa. Would you like a cup o' tea?'

George declined. It was one of his tactics not to get too familiar with the clients. He quickly surveyed the room as was his wont, in order to get an impression of who this woman was. It was excessively tidy and clean, with flowers, and lots of photos of a child, a Yorkshire calendar, a large mirror dead centre above the fireplace. A large white cat sat on the windowsill outside.

'Are you all right with cats, love? I put her outside just in case'

'Absolutely', said George, 'I am definitely a cat person.'

He smiled at Mary, who immediately felt at home with him. The language of cat tails was something they had in common. She had vacced the sofa before he came just in case. The only thing out of place was a boy of about nine who was asleep on the floor beside the sofa. He decided not to say anything

George reached in his case and got out his notebook and pen.

'Is it all right if I make a few notes, Mrs Brown?'

'That's fine. You can call me Mary, if you like.'

'Ok Mary. Would you like to tell me about the situation with you and your neighbour? How long have you been here?'

The story began to unfold. Fifteen years here, ten with her first husband, and two with the present partner, who only came at weekends, and occasionally during the week. Just the one child. She liked order and tidiness, but since the new neighbour came along two years ago, things had changed a lot. There was careless parking, cigarette smoke coming over the garden fence when her washing was out, loud singing to the radio, shouting, laughing, loud phone calls.

'And...' she paused, and reached down to place her hand over the boy's ear. 'SEXUAL NOISES,' she mouthed quietly, turning her face away from George. 'Late at night, when he's asleep. His bedroom is right next to theirs, and it wakes him up you see. Then he comes into my bedroom and wakes me up.'

'I see,' said George, in a completely disinterested tone, that he practised for just such occasions, trying not to smile.

'And how often are they, er...' Start again George. 'How often does this happen, Mary?'

'Oh, every weekend, and sometimes on a weekday as well. Sometimes IN THE DAY TIME too!'

'Really!' said George, in the tone of a doctor about to make a diagnosis. He was already looking forward to meeting this neighbour.

Mary had become so relaxed with this man, despite, or perhaps because of, his professional manner, that she felt she could talk her life away now. She went on to tell him what he already knew, that she and her partner were quiet orderly people, who liked things to be the way they used to be. She was greatly relieved to get it all out in the open in front of someone she was sure would understand, and want to help to put things right. George let her ramble on, although he had long ago stopped taking notes.

'Shall I tell you what will happen next, Mary?'

He gently launched into the scenario where after he had met the neighbour, if they all agreed he would organise a room where they could meet, and put things right between them.

Mary was rather dubious about the latter, but George, used to almost every client telling him that it wouldn't work, persuaded her to give it a try. They shook hands, and he left with a professional blank face, to make a few more notes in his car.

*

'Andy!'

'Wassup?'

'Get off me!'

'What for?'

'I think there's someone at the door.'

'Aw bloody 'ell. Ignore 'em.'

'No, I can't. I just remembered. That bloke from mediation. It'll be him.'

'Mediation? What the hell's that?'

Tracey shoved him over and grabbed a tee shirt and jeans, and lolloped over to the window. George was waiting outside the front door.

'Can you come round to the back, love,' she shouted through the window. As she made for the door of the bedroom, she said 'You stay 'ere love, I'll be back for more later.'

*

George made his way past Mary's window and out of the corner of his eye caught a glimpse of her peeping behind the lace curtain. Round the very tidy garden and at the back towards Tracey's back yard, which was not.

Tracey's lawn, if it could be called that, was like a little jungle, in which grew some uncut long grass, lots of dandelions, several beer bottles, a pizza box, and a sagging washing line on two poles. The gate didn't quite close, and as he was fiddling with it, Tracey came to the back door and said, 'It's all right love, just leave it. Come on in.'

He made his way gingerly past a basket of washing, and parts of an old bike which obstructed the entrance to the kitchen. A large and very old black Labrador lay across the entrance to the lounge, which he nearly tripped over. It raised itself with some effort and shoved its nose into George's crotch by way of greeting.

"Enry give over!' said Tracey, giving the dog a huge shove. 'Sit down love,' she said to George, grabbing hold of some magazines, a cigarette packet, and a man's jumper which lay over the sofa. A very large flat screen TV over the fireplace was showing East Enders.

As he sat down, Henry came back and lay his chin on George's knees, wagging a weak tail and looking up at him adoringly. George opened his case to get out his notebook, and the dog transferred its face to the bag and started to snuffle.

"Enry! Give up! I hope you don't mind dogs, do you love. 'E's just a bit too friendly.'

'No, I'm fine, Mrs er,' George was just a little bit un-fine.

'Just call me Tracey, all right?'

'Yes, and I'm George,' he managed a smile, and shuffled a little way down the sofa to try to regain a little dignity.

'What's this all about then?' She sounded genuinely puzzled. 'I had this letter from the council about her next door. What's she been sayin'?

'Well, I've just been to see your neighbour, but we don't normally tell you what the other person says. I'm just here to listen. Would you like to tell me what is the situation between you and your neighbour?'

Tracey started to search for a lighter, as she picked up the cigarettes she had rescued from the sofa.

'I'm sorry Tracey, but would you mind switching off the TV for a bit. I find it hard to concentrate.'

Tracey gave him a funny look, but reached for the remote, and turned down the sound, but not the vision. He didn't feel like asking for more.

'Situation? There isn't any situation as far as I know. I hardly ever see the woman. What's she been sayin?'

George had learned over the years not to use the word 'problem', as it immediately left the assumption in the mind of the neighbour that there was one.

'Have you been having any differences of opinion with your neighbour?'

'Not that I'm aware of love. She hardly ever speaks to me.'

'Have you not had any conversation with her recently?'

'No love, she keeps herself to herself like. I hardly know she's 'ere most of the time. See her little boy sometimes goin' to school. An' I think she has a man what comes round now an' then. And I've not spoken to him either.'

'But you've had a letter from the council, haven't you.

Could you tell me what it says?'

'I'll get it for you.' And she searches for some time amongst a pile of old envelopes behind an ornament on the windowsill. 'Here it is, have a look for yourself.'

George takes out the letter. It simply mentions a complaint from a neighbour about noise, and a request to accept mediation.

'What would you say the noise is that this letter refers to, Tracey?'

'Well, the dog barks in the morning when postman comes. An' I like singin' to the radio or CDs now an' then.'

'Tell me a bit about your routines. Would you say you are a morning or a night person for instance?'

What the bloody 'ell is 'e on about? thinks Tracey. 'Well, I have a part time job, some afternoons and some nights like, is that what you mean?'

'And what time do you go to bed normally?'

'It depends what time I get home don't it.' She is thinking, *that's bloody obvious int it?*

'Is it just yourself here most of the time?'

'No, I have a partner who comes round now and then. An' me son comes round some weekends with his girlfriend. And a few friends, like.'

George thinks he hears the sound of a toilet being flushed upstairs.

'Can I ask what sort of things you do when you have people round?'

George was searching for some clue as to what Mary had told him, without seeming to be rude.

'Well, you know, we like to party now an' then, have a

few jars, bit o' music, like. What do you like to do?' Tracey looks at the serious face of George and has real difficulty imagining what he might like to do.

'So might it be the times when you have friends round when things get a bit noisy perhaps?'

'Yeah, why not. That's how we are!'

'And you've never heard your neighbour say anything about that?'

'Nah. She never show her face round here like.'

George has got the picture, but not the crucial bit, which he is not going to mention. Having gained a little bit of ground he then goes into the routine about arranging a meeting in another place. She is surprisingly compliant, and gently pushing the dog's nose from his lap, he gets up and thanks her, and keeping his face straight gingerly makes his way out through the kitchen and garden to his car, where he smiles and blows a sigh of relief.

Tracey meanwhile makes her way thoughtfully back upstairs, then bursts open the bedroom door. 'Nah then love, where were we?'

*

Richard and Mary sit upright and uptight at the table George has carefully arranged in the community centre. Richard doesn't really want to be there, but Mary had asked if he could come for a bit of moral support (moral being the operative word). George has put the kettle on and they are already into their first cup of tea, since they came ten minutes early, as Mary doesn't like to be late.

George has a repertoire of neutral small talk he keeps for such occasions, which keep some distance away from the topic in hand. All the same, his stock of topics is wearing thin by the time Andy and Tracey roll up ten minutes late.

They sort of fall in the door backwards in the middle of a chat with some friends who happen to be passing by outside. 'Right love, We'll sees you later, all right? After this is over.' They wind up with a saucy laugh, and Tracey totters over to the table on very high heels and very tight jeans.

'Ello love, how you doin', all right?'

She greets the couple with a grin, and looks at Richard quizzically, like a specimen in a glass case she has never seen before. He stands up and offers his hand to both of them, which they grab uncomfortably, not used to such formality. There is a strong odour of cigarettes and beer, which discomforts Mary and Richard.

George thanks them for coming and offers them some tea and biscuits. 'Nah, you're all right love,' says Tracey, 'we've just been, er… haven't we Andy.'

'Yeah,' says Andy, who also doesn't want to be here, but was cajoled into it by Tracey. The two men sit staring at the table.

'Shall we make a start then,' says George, and goes into his routine about the conduct of mediation, including a recent rule about social media, which has lately become the villain of many a case.

'Mary, would you like to begin, please?'

Mary has in front of her a list of items, which she had prepared earlier in case she forgot anything.

'Well, I really don't want to upset you Tracey, but...'

'I tell you what's upsettin' love, it's gettin' letters from the council,' Tracey butts in. George quickly intervenes to remind her of the rule he had just laid out a minute ago about 'uninterrupted time.'

'Well, I mean...' she goes on, but George stops her again. 'You will get your own time in a few minutes, if you'd just like to listen quietly for a bit, OK?'

Tracey doing anything quietly doesn't come naturally, but she crosses her legs and turns slightly away from the table, staring out of the window.

Mary continues. 'It's when I'm sitting in the garden, or when me washing's out, and the cigarette smoke... you see, me and Richard are not smokers, and it sort of makes the washing smell, if you know what I mean.'

Tracey casts a rye glance at Andy, who raises an eyebrow and wrinkles his brow.

'And then it's the music, and the parties, you know, we used to have such a quiet life, and now it's all changed. And sometimes, I can hear every word you're saying on the phone.'

Mary is not used to complaining out loud, and feels very uncomfortable not just at having to say these things, but at having to upset someone else. She almost feels guilty, although she and Richard spend a good deal of time complaining in private. She looks at him appealingly, hoping he might speak up in her defence.

'Richard,' says George, 'is there anything you would like to add?'

'Well, it's like Mary says,' he mumbles, 'I've heard it

myself when Tracey's on the phone, it's sort of embarrassing, like we're spying on someone.'

George briefly tries to summarise what he has heard so far. 'I believe when we spoke before you talked about some other noises?'

Mary wants to sink through the floor.

'It's sort of late at night, when my little boy's asleep, and it wakes him up, and he comes into our room to tell me… about the… about the sounds coming from your bedroom Tracey. And not just at night either.'

She has managed to say it without using any rude words.

Andy and Tracey share a look and a grin that says, *'Now I wonder what that could be?'*

'I think what Mary means is the sounds of your love making, would that be right, Mary?'

Mary nods. She and Richard stare at the table.

George sums up again and then passes the baton to Tracey and Andy.

Although Tracey is a bit of a wild child, she also has a heart of gold, and likes to be open about everything. So, although her instinct is to mock at people like these who are so quiet and careful, she decides to go easy on them.

'You know love, I hardly know you're there half the time. If I knew you didn't like cigarette smoke I might a done summat about it. But you never said owt did you. How was I to know?'

Mary nods anxiously.

'I suppose I ought to notice when your washing's out, and I could try not to smoke then. But if we have friends round in the summer we want to be in the garden like, and

I can't ask them all not to smoke, can I?'

Mary shakes her head.

'And the way I talk, like, it's how I am, y' know, it's how I've always been since I were a little lass. We were a big family, and you had to shout to be noticed, no-wot-a-mean?'

Mary nods, and a small smile creeps onto her face.

'I don't mind you hearing me on the phone. I don't have any secrets love. What you see is what you get, see. You understand?'

Richard even begins to smile here, and a knowing glance passes between him and Andy, who raises his eyebrows in acknowledgment.

Tracey thinks she could expand her personality profile a bit further, and have a bit of fun.

'Now then. Them noises you're hearing late at night. would that be when Andy's here, do you think love?'

'Yes, I suppose so,' Mary offers sheepishly, knowing damn fine it is.

'And on a weekend as well? Like when we're both not working?'

'And sometimes during the week as well.'

'You know, when I get home after work, or when he comes home, we're not tired like most folk. We're that pleased to see each other, and full of energy, and he's such a randy sod, no-wot-a-mean?'

She flashes a look at Andy, who by this time is smiling broadly, as is Richard too.

'Come on, you are aren't you love!' He nods enthusiastically.

'And ah tell you, when I wanna ravish him I'm gonna ravish him, no-wat-a-mean!'

'I think we know what you mean, Tracey,' says George, and letting go of all professional decorum he laughs along with the two men and Tracey, and even Mary is forced to admit a broad smile. The ice is broken at last. And Richard is thinking, *By heck, I could do with a bit o' that.*

George quietly makes a note of Tracey's last remark, to keep for later use.

'Is there anything you could do, Tracey to make things better for Mary and Richard?'

Richard thinks to himself, *I could send her round to Tracey's for a few lessons!*

'Well,' says Tracey, 'I don't think I could ever do it quietly like, what do you think Andy?' She throws him a dirty look.

'No,' says Andy, 'she's right there. Once she gets going there's no holding her back. She's like a bloody tornado!'

By now the atmosphere has lightened so much that they all sit around laughing heartily.

'I think thee and me, Mary, need to get together and have a little chat about our sex lives, what you say, eh?'

Yeeeaaay! thinks Richard.

'An' that lad or yours, Richard, I think you and him need a little chat about birds an' bees, no-wot-a-mean?'

'I think I do, love,' Richard nods, 'an' we can move him into the other room, Mary, so 'e's not so close to the action.'

Another burst of laughter round the table.

'An' if I were you love,' says Tracey, 'I'd tell him to shut up and put up, and put his head under the pillow! Then you won't get woken up so often.'

George senses the meeting drawing to an end.

'Tracey, what do you think Mary could do if she feels she needs to tell you something?'

'Well just come an' tell me love. I'll not bite your head off you know.'

'Shall I knock on your front door?' Mary is struggling with the idea of a streak of informality bursting into her ordered life.

'No love, just come round 't back an' shout over 't fence like everyone else. Nobody uses front door round 'ere.'

'OK then.'

'Don't write to 't bloody council. I don't want any more o' them letters through 't door, all right?'

'All right,' says Mary. 'I'm really sorry to upset you, Tracey.'

After a short summing up, George asks them to have some tea while he writes up an agreement, which he does with a smile on his face. One of the spicier documents he has ever had to write.

The two men chat over tea and biscuits about kids and football and car parking, and anything other than sex, while Tracey sits closer to Mary like a mother comforting a sad daughter. As they get up to go, she gives her a big hug. When they leave it is with a lighter step and a lot of laughter. George closes the door behind them, goes back to the table to finish his notes, but finds himself unable to do anything until he has stopped giggling.

Takeaway

The days were too long for Sharon. She felt as if there was something she ought to be doing, her brain itched for it, but as yet, no-one had been able to show her what it was. It wasn't school, although the free school meals just about kept her alive. Her mates were most of them there, especially at lunch time and after school, but it was the bits in between she couldn't cope with.

She had a very selective take on the curriculum. Anything before eleven was no good. Anything involving shorts and tee shirts and running and jumping was pants. All the schools in the area seemed to be sited in wide open spaces subject to arctic winds. And showering was only for idiots. The only human beings allowed access to her body were tattooists and piercers. And, oh, there was her step brother Zak, but he didn't count, being welded to his computer nine tenths of the time. But at least he shared her view of education.

Dad was on nights. What he did she wasn't exactly sure. But he was good for the odd fiver now and then. They both slept in the mornings, and by the time he woke up Sharon had sloped off to school, or somewhere. He didn't ask too much. She didn't say too much. It was better that way. She hung out with friends after school, and by the time she came home he was either off to the pub, or asked her to go out for a takeaway, which they shared in silence in front of the telly.

So, then there was the whole of the evening to fill. Zak would be zooming in and out of some virtual reality zone, or gaming with some other geek on the other side of the world. She had not yet succumbed to the boyfriend girlfriend thing, although she knew some of her mates would be hard at it most nights, in secret places, or in one or the other's back bedrooms, doing their 'homework' on human biology.

But she was no innocent. She and Zak would occasionally gawk at the various styles of copulation available on different porn sites he was familiar with. They mostly seemed to consist of grunting inarticulate men with huge cocks and no faces, humping endlessly a parade of young and seemingly innocent girls, in bizarre positions on the edge of kitchen worktops or caught in the middle of a workout in the gym. The men could go for hours without ejaculation, and the women shrieked and howled with ecstasy for minutes on end.

Sharon tried to imagine her friends doing it with any of the spotty and smelly dorks who inhabited the high school and lurked on street corners near her house. But somehow the images wouldn't come. She and Zak had even tried out some of these techniques themselves, but usually ended up in an embarrassing mess or in hoots of laughter.

It was a text on her cheap and crappy phone that led her one night to the Asian takeaway a few streets away with a bunch of bored girls like herself. Free chips they said. The telly was always on. There was a sporadic influx of kids and adults waiting for a pizza or a curry, which they would eat on the street, or take home, or sit and chew at one of the formica tables. That way she often got to share someone's meal, or just sat and enjoyed the constant rude and humorous banter with some of her mates, mostly girls like her, with nothing better to do. It was loud, smelly and lively, and she loved it.

When trade was a bit slack one or two of the men behind the counter would come and sit with them and chat them up and make them laugh. There was Omar and Ali and Zafar. They would bring odd snacks from the fry ups, onion bhajis or samosas to nibble. Even a can of coke or a chocolate bar. It was so spontaneous and thoughtful. The girls were impressed. Like Sharon most of them had no experience of being given so much attention. She even managed to take home a few freebies to share with Zak.

One night it was Omar who suggested she and he might go to a film on at the Odeon. Dad's largesse and time was limited, and cinema had not been on the menu for a few years, not since Mum had left him in fact. So, Sharon agreed, even though Omar was at least ten years older than her. 'I 'aven't got much to wear,' she told him. 'Me dad's a bit of a skinflint.' 'That's ok love,' said Omar. 'Just come as you are.'

So, they did. Omar was thoughtful and considerate, bought her popcorn and a drink, and behaved impeccably.

She put her arm in his as they left, and thanked him as she left his car, when he had driven her home. She felt good.

'Where've you been?' asked Zak as she rolled in late that night. He was still in zombie land, but noticed her slipping past into the bathroom.

'Out,' she offered.

'You're a bit late like'

'So?' She challenged from behind the bathroom door. 'You're not me Dad you know!'

'Yeah, but takeaway's closed now innit?'

'I've not been in't takeaway.'

'Been at someone's 'ouse then?' he persisted.

'No! Bloody'ell! If you must know I've been to't pictures'

''Oo with, one o' your mates then?'

'Yeah. One o' me mates. That satisfy you?'

'Anyone I know?'

'Who do you know then?'

'Someone wi' a car, then. I saw you get out'

'So. What if I did? What's it to you?'

'Someone old enough to drive, eh?'

'What is this? You Sherlock Holmes or summat?'

'It were a man, werent' it'

'Yeah, it were a man, all right?'

'Ya wanna watch it you, love. Nobody I know's got a car.'

Zak was showing more than the usual concern for his sister, who was in fact his best mate. A little bit jealous.

Sharon brushed her teeth, and slid into bed with a smile. It were a good night out.

*

She woke at about eleven the following morning. Down to the kitchen in her pyjamas to see if there was anything to eat in the cupboard or the fridge. At the bottom of the stairs she saw a letter at the front door. It was addressed to Mr J Taylor, her dad. On the back was the rubber-stamped address of her school.

Finding some Rice Krispies but no milk, she poured herself a dish full and began to eat them dry. She tore open the letter, and screwed her dry eyes open enough to read it.

'Dear Mr Taylor, It has come to our notice that your daughter Sharon has not been in full attendance at school for several weeks now. We would like to discuss this with you both, and would be grateful if you would kindly make an appointment to speak to me after school in the next few days. Or at another time of your choosing. Yours sincerely – (Head of year)'

Finishing her cereal, Sharon ripped up the letter, and on her way to school, dropped it in the river.

*

'Where were you last night Sharon? We missed you.'

The usual gang were gathered around the tables at the takeaway.

'Where was Omar too? Was it 'is night off then?'

A cackle of laughter and a big 'Ooooooh!' They had put two and two together.

'What's it to you then?'

Sharon was on the defensive, but at the same time felt a certain pride. Apart from the odd scuffle in the corridors at school, and a few lewd remarks, and her very private relationship with Zak, she had never been out with a boy alone, without the company of a whole gang of kids. She still had pimples, and was dotted with piercings in her nose and eyebrows. A slash of red dye in her hair was her most adventurous move into young adulthood so far.

'You know how old 'e is?'

Tracey was half envious, but a mite concerned as well.

'Yeah,' they all chipped in at once.

''E's gotta be twenty-one at least. You wanna watch your step love.'

'Ow old 'e is as nowt to do wi you lot,' Sharon said, ''E's a very nice bloke. An' it were a good film too.'

'Did you get to watch any of it then?' Fern chipped in, and this gave rise to a bubble of obscenities and sniggers.

'You mind your own damn business. Go and get your own boyfriends if you wanna find out!'

Sharon was on a roll and was not going to share any information when she knew she had the upper hand. Life was shitty enough for all of them she knew. And a bit of one upmanship was a new experience for her. She was enjoying it.

*

Over the next few weeks, the takeaway experience continued. There were jokes and familiarities with the men from the business. They were liberal with the freebies, and most of the girls stuck with it. It was more attention than they got at home or at school, and for some, the food was more than welcome. One or two others got taken out to the cinema, to discos and other treats. Omar tried it on with a few others, but he kept coming back to Sharon. He made her feel special.

One evening he was watching her fiddling with her mobile, noticing she was obviously not happy with it.

'You had that a long time then?' he asked.

'Yeah. Too bloody long, she said, 'Its useless'

'Would you like another one?'

'Yeah, course I would, but me Dad can't afford it.'

'I can get you one. Cheap.' He smiled.

'Nooo, you don't wanna do that. They're expensive.' She said, unconvincingly. She desperately wanted a new one.

'I'll see what I can do. Watch this space,' he said. Her eyes lit up.

*

'Ah, Sharon.' Mr Spencer, the Year Head, caught up with her in a corridor one afternoon, as she was about to slope off for a cig behind the gym.

'Can you spare a minute please?'

'What's it about?' she said, irritated with herself for allowing him to catch up with her.

'I sent a letter to your dad last week. Did he tell you?'

'No. He ain't said owt.'

'Well, I wanted to have a word with him and yourself.' Spencer knew not to say what it was for.

'Me dad works nights, an' 'e's asleep most o't mornin'' she offered, hoping this would put him off.

'Is he around in the afternoons then?'

'I dunno, cos I'm here, aren't I,' she tried to put some conviction in her voice.

'Well, that's what I wanted to talk to you about,' said Spencer, but stopped himself before going any further. 'Do you think you could ask him when you get home? I really would like to talk to him.'

'If he's there I'll ask him tonight,' she said with a sigh.

'Thank you, Sharon.' And he walked off briskly like a man on a mission.

'Oh shit!' she whispered to herself.

*

Zak was also on a mission of his own. At seventeen he was the son of his dad's first wife, with no other siblings than Sharon, and few friends. But his mother had been a very bright woman, and he had inherited her intelligence. He had no intention of spending his adult life working in a factory like his dad.

Like Sharon he had found the life of school irksome and boring, and his last two years there were part time and choosy. He was brilliant at maths, science and computer studies, and in the latter found himself streets ahead of the school staff. He had hacked into the school system without their knowledge, and was able to slide into college life with a little manipulation. He attended those sections of the computer course that interested him the most, and made up for the rest by dint of his ability to figure things out with his laser sharp intellect.

With no documentation from his early life, he had found a way to forge a birth certificate, and by lying about his age and with a nod from his dad, he had got himself a bank account. He was also knee deep into the murky pool of bit coins and other virtual currencies. His home computer and printer were state of the art, and how he obtained them was a mystery to his dad, who asked no questions, but admired from a distance.

Sharon was aware of her brother's dark arts, but was canny enough not to enquire too deeply, but to blackmail him into coughing up a bit of cash now and again in exchange for her silence. So, although their domestic routines left a lot to be desired, and none of them could cook, she managed to salvage a bit of street cred with a few of life's essentials, such as her various piercings and hair colour and cool jeans.

When Zak caught sight of her new phone, he was curious.

'Where'd' you get that then?'

'None of your business,' she snarled.

'I could 'ave got you a better one.'

'When I want one, I'll let you know then.'

'Does it 'ave a decent camera?'

'S'all right.'

'Let us 'ave a look then.'

In a moment of weakness, she handed it to him. In a few seconds he had found some pictures of her mates at the takeaway, gurning and larking about, mouths full of chips. There was also a young man caught in a selfie with Sharon.

'Who's he then?'

Sharon snatched it off him, embarrassed. 'Nobody you know!'

She didn't want him to see the next few pictures.

'I could get you a better camera if you like,' said Zak, who had guessed at something she didn't want him to know about, something that alarmed him.

'One that's not so obvious, y' know, like, one that you don't want anyone to see?'

'Why would I need that then?'

Sharon picked up on a note of warning in his voice.

'There's stuff on the internet that spies use, y'know, like what you can wear in your hair or your ears, or your belly button,' he added, guessing where she might be leading herself. 'Interested?'

'I might be,' she sneered uncertainly, 'just fer a laugh like.'

'OK.'

*

'Wanna come to a party?'

Omar was in a sparky mood, surrounded by half a dozen teenage girls, and off duty tonight at the takeaway.

'What, now?' said Sharon, 'Yeah, why not?'

They all piled into his bright red Audi, most of them squashed into the back seat without seat belts, and Sharon in front. He roared off with a squeal of tyres at break neck speed through the quiet and pot holed streets of the little town. In a few minutes they were in a district that Sharon knew about but none of them had ever ventured. He pulled up at the back of a large Victorian terraced house with expensive cast iron railings painted gold at the tips, and a stone lion standing guard at the gate.

Loud rock music filled the air, rumbling out of an upstairs window, behind which coloured lights flashed on and off. The girls looked at each other for a moment, and all decided without a second thought, to run up the drive and into the door held open by Omar, and up the stairs. There was gold flock wall paper and a smell not unlike that of the takeaway.

The room upstairs was thick with smoke and a strange sweet smell she thought she recognised. The lights were off, but disco lights flashed on and off in time with the music. There were several girls of Sharon's age, some of whom she knew from school. There were about a dozen men, some of whom she recognised from the takeaway, and some older ones. Most of them were swaying and bumping to the music, some with their arms around a girl, and a few seated in corners with a girl on their knee. Some were sharing cigarettes, and some were sharing girls.

There was booze, cans of lager and beer, stacked on a table in the corner, and empty cans lying around on the floor, the mantelpiece and fireplace. Both men and girls were well tanked up, loud and happy, and they shouted at the new arrivals to join them. Omar grabbed Sharon around the waist, and held her tightly, rubbing himself against her, and other men did the same with Sharon's friends, as they swayed and rocked to the beat. Sharon had little choice but to go with the flow, and very soon they melted into one big body, laughing, singing and grinding, with no idea of time or place. She was given cans of lager, and shared a smoke with Omar and other men, until she was aware of a strange sensation of floating above the crowd, as the music seemed to shrink into the background.

How long this went on for she was unaware, it could have been hours, but it was a blissful state to be in and she felt ridiculously happy. People came and went to the bathroom, and in and out of other rooms. At one point she was aware of lying down in a different room, and someone was lying very close, removing her jeans. She found this enormously funny and giggled uncontrollably for a long time. There seemed to be others lying nearby, who were all in a similar state, some completely naked. Some were back in the disco room with no clothes on, and some were in the bathroom being sick. And at some point, after a complete blank spell she found herself in the car again.

*

'Hello?'

There was a persistent knocking at the front door. Jim Taylor had not been long awake, and was in no fit state for visitors.

'Hello? Mr Taylor?'

Jim grunted, and hurriedly removed the remains of last night's takeaway from the table, and put some empty lager cans in the bin. He stumbled to the front door. 'Who is it?'

'It's Mr Spencer, from the school.'

Spencer? Spencer? Don't know any Spencer. He took the

chain off the lock and opened the door.

'Sorry to bother you, Mr Taylor. May we come in please?'

'What's it about?'

'We'd like to have a word about your Sharon, Mr Taylor, if that's all right'

Jim moved out of the way and Spencer and a woman came in and stood awkwardly in the hallway.

'This is Miss Jenkins, Sharon's form teacher'

'Right, come on in. I'm afraid I'm only just up, not expecting visitors. I work nights, you know.' Jim was feeling awkward and apprehensive. 'Shall I put kettle on?'

'No that's Ok Mr Taylor, thank you.'

Jim brushed off a chair and pulled up three unmatching ones around the table.

'Is Sharon here at the moment?'

'I don't think so,' said Jim, 'In't she at school then?'

'No, Mr Taylor, that's why we have come. I sent you a letter recently, but you didn't reply. I also asked Sharon to tell you we wanted to see you.'

'Well, no I aven't had no letter, and Sharon din't say owt, like.'

'Mr Taylor,' Miss Jenkins spoke up, 'your Sharon has not been at registration in the mornings for quite a while now, but she is seen at some lessons in the afternoon. Did you know this?'

'Well, our Sharon's a bit like me, can't get up in't morning.'

'Do you know where she goes to when she's not at school, Mr Taylor?'

'Can't say I do, love. I wake up generally about now, and

she's not here. I thought she'd be at school, y'know.'

Spencer waded in. 'You know your Sharon is quite a bright girl. She's in her GCSE years and she should be able to get a few good results. But at the present rate that doesn't look like its likely to happen. Is she doing any homework, do you know?'

Jim smiled, remembering his own aversion to that particular form of punishment.

'You see, I'm on nights, and by't time she gets home, I'm about ready to go out. Can't say I ever see 'er doin' any work like.'

'When you say 'she gets home', do you mean she doesn't come home straight after school?'

'Well, no, she's off wi'er mates, like most lasses these days. You know 'ow it is, don't you?'

'I'm beginning to think I do,' said Spencer coldly. 'Mr Taylor, I think your Sharon is a cause for concern.'

*

On the night of the party, Zak noticed she was not home when he went to bed late, but that was not unusual for Sharon.

In the morning around eleven he made his way bleary eyed downstairs, to find her curled up on the floor at the foot of the stairs.

'Oh bloody 'ell!' He gave her a gentle kick. She didn't stir. He bent down over her. She was a funny colour.

'Sharon?' No response.

'Sharon!' What to do now.

She was too big for him to pick her up, but he couldn't leave her there. He managed to lever her into a sitting position, sat on the bottom step and manoeuvred her onto his lap, got her arms round his neck, and began slowly to shuffle backwards up the stairs. Unused to so much physical activity he sat with her on the top step for a long time. She felt cold. He hugged her closer, and without thinking he gently kissed her forehead. He remained there some while with tears in his eyes. Then he dragged her backwards across the floor and heaved her up on to the bed. Laying her out straight, he pulled the quilt over her. He went to his own room and took his quilt and double wrapped her.

He felt her pulse in her neck. As much as he knew about such things it felt normal to him. She was not hot. Just zonked. Seeing the band around her neck with the little jewel at the front he remembered. He lifted up her head and gently unclasped it. He took it to his room and switched on his computer.

*

There was another banging on the door next afternoon. Jim looked out of the window and saw a police car parked nearby.

'Mr Jim Taylor?'

They sat at his little table, the two police officers seeming to take up an enormous amount of room with their waistcoats stuffed with phones, and all the paraphernalia of security on the streets. There was a little flashing light and some clicks and buzzes while they talked. Jim was not comfortable.

'Is your daughter here, sir?'

'No, she should be at school, shouldn't she?'

'Don't you know then, Mr Taylor?'

Telling them the tale of his late nights and sleeping habits again was beginning to sound a bit weak, even to Jim.

'Why, has summat 'appened?' He felt a sudden tightening in his chest, and his mouth went dry.

'Something's happened, Mr Taylor, but we're not quite sure what it is. I'm afraid your daughter's in hospital.'

'In 'ospital? Bloody 'ell. What's goin' on?'

Jim was scared. The years of scraping a living and trying to cope with two sullen teenagers and not knowing half the time where they were, suddenly felt like a great big lump in his head.

'She's all right, Mr Taylor, not in any danger as I understand. But we would like you to come to the station with us if you wouldn't mind.'

'What for? I 'aven't done owt.'

'No, sir, you're not being charged with anything. But there's something we need to show you before you go to see your daughter. Is your son in, by the way?'

'N-no, 'e's at college. ''E should be at college I think.'

'You think, Mr Taylor. Don't you know?'

'This is 'ow it is 'ere. They both come and go as they please. 'alf the time I don't know where they are, but they've not been in any trouble before. What's goin' on?'

'I can't really tell you just now, sir, but if you'll come with us, you'll find out soon enough.'

*

They took him down several bleak and disinfectant scented corridors to a bleak and stuffy little room at the back of the station. They asked for a tea tray to be delivered. There was a computer on the desk. They waited in silence while the woman police officer poured some teas and coffees and offered him some biscuits.

'We'd like you to watch this video, Mr Taylor. I have to warn you it's not very nice. We think it's come from your son. He told us he will be with Sharon at the hospital.

Jim watched in silence as a shaky procession of young men and girls dancing and kissing amid flashing lights and very loud music filled the screen. At some points there were close ups of someone's neck and hairy chest. After about five minutes, the policeman stopped it, and fast forwarded to another scene in another room.

'The dancing went on for some time, Mr Taylor, but we want you to see what happened next.'

What happened next was so revolting, that Jim vomited without warning onto the floor, and felt his stomach turn to water.

'Is... is that our Sharon then, is that 'er... under that... that bloke, all them blokes? Jesus Christ!'

'We think it is, sir. That's what your son says. He says he has proof.'

'Was 'e there as well? 'E don't go to discos, dammit'

'No, sir, He wasn't. But if you're feeling all right, we'll take you to the hospital now.'

*

The Facebook page of the Shangri La takeaway had a section in which customers could 'rate our service.' Not normally noticed by most customers, who were just passing by for a quick snack, all of a sudden there was a succession of photos on the page of young men dancing and kissing young girls. 'Our staff like to keep our customers satisfied,' it said. They were named, and a link was added. 'Follow this link to see how well we are doing.' The link led to a video.

That night the police raided the takeaway, cleared out the young girls, took them off for questioning, and arrested the staff. Soon after its windows were smashed by an angry crowd, who also targeted a number of similar takeaways in the town. It was several days before the police managed to settle things down.

*

Sharon rather liked her new home. It was clean, she had a bigger room, with her own computer, and overlooked a lovely garden. Her foster parents, Dave and Sheila, had two other children, a little younger than Sharon, and two energetic dogs, that took to her straight away, and needed feeding and walking on a regular basis. The kitchen was always well stocked with nutritious food, and Sheila cooked most days. There were no takeaways.

Although she was in another town, Zak was able to see her quite often, and they were in daily touch on the even more hi-tech phone he had given her. Dave took her and the other girls to school every day, and collected her at the end, although he was careful not to drive too close to the school, so she would not be embarrassed.

The new school were careful to place her in a form group with a solicitous form teacher, and a peer group who kept in touch, and invited her to their homes on a regular basis. No piercings or jewellery were allowed. She resumed her studies, and soon found she actually liked working, although she would not say as much to any of her new mates. She had a bit of a thing about cooking, which she had never done before, but with Sheila's help she soon found out that a curry you make yourself is so much cheaper and tastier than a takeaway. She even began to enjoy playing girls' football, where her natural cunning and ripe vocabulary seemed to be an advantage.

Breaking it gently

Listen son, you know I've been on my own for half of your life, since your mum left us. That must feel like ages to you.

Yeah, says Jake, but she hasn't left *me*, has she.

No. I know what you mean, 'cos you see her twice a week, and some weekends. And you still have grandma to give us a break.

So, you've not been on your own, have you Dad. You've got me and Jodie, and grandma, haven't you.

Dad smiles. Yes, but what I mean is, what I need is, like, you have your sister, your mum and your friends, don't you. You need them, don't you.

Yeah, I suppose so. Jake has never thought about that need word.

So, not much has really changed for you. You've still got the people you most need in your life. But I haven't, have I.

Why not? Don't you need us?

Yes, but I don't have anyone my age, know what I mean. When you're grown up, you'll need more than just your mum and your sister. You'll need someone to, er…

To sleep with? Jake grins.

Well yes. It's not nice sleeping on your own.

Why not? I sleep on my own. Jodie sleeps on her own.

What I mean is, you need someone your own age, to love, you know, to love.

Don't you love us then? Jake says with a frown.

Course I do, but everyone loves their kids. But its not like having someone…

To sleep with?

No. Someone to call… your partner. A man, a woman, they have a special relationship, more important than anything else.

You mean we're not important then?

No. You know that's not what I mean. You will always be important to me. Look, what I'm trying to tell you is… I met Farida, a few years ago, at the community centre, when we were helping to look after asylum seekers and refugees.

She's a… a refugee, like, a foreigner?

Yes, she is. But that's not important. She's a human being, and she's really nice, and in the last year or two we've become really close…

You been seeing her then? You kept that close. When were you seeing her?

That's not important. The thing is, I really love her. I think you would like her.

Is she gonna be your special partner then? What colour is she?

She's sort of, golden brown, like an English person with a sun tan. She's from Iraq.

Mum won't like that.

Mum and I, we… We don't agree on many things. She's got a… a friend, and I…

She's got a boy-friend? Who's he?

She may not have introduced you yet. You see it's really difficult, in our situation, knowing when to change things. We think about you and Jodie, and we know you like things to stay the same. But… it gets lonely.

But you've got us. How can you be lonely?

It's not the same thing Jake. Mum and I we used to love each other, and that's where you and Jodie came from. But after a while we stopped loving each other, and well, you maybe don't remember, we used to argue and shout, and so she left, and made us both lonely.

Is Farida your 'girl-friend' then?

Yes. You could say that. Would you like to meet her?

I dunno. What would Mum say?

What do you think? Mum and I are divorced. We can see whoever we like. I don't want to hurt her. But I don't have to ask her permission.

What about Jodie? Have you told her?

Not yet. But I thought… one at a time, like. I will talk to her later. I just wanted you to know. You can tell her if you like.

Jake sighs and looks at his feet.

Are we gonna meet her then, this Farida? When.

She has two young boys. And she doesn't have any relatives to look after them. But she asked if we could go to her house and she will cook for us. What do you think?

Does she cook foreign stuff?

Of course. It's really good!
Have you been there already?
Yes.
A lot!
Yes.
Jake lets this sink in.
Oh.
You know, the times when you and Jodie have been at your mum's...
You went to her's?
Yes.
What are they like, her kids?
Just like you, only a slightly different colour. And a bit naughty, just like you. Similar age to you too. You could be friends.
Would they come here?
If you like. But let's do one thing at a time eh?
Jake smiles.
OK.

Later.
Dad?
What love.
Is it true?
Is what true?
What Jake said.
What did he say?
About you and this – woman.
You mean, me and Farida.
Yeah. Is that her name?

That's right. Yes, it is true.

You mean every time we go to Mum's, you and her…

Well not every time, but whenever we can.

That's a bit sneaky, isn't it? I mean…

Don't you have any secrets then? What about your, er, boyfriend?

I haven't got a boyfriend!

I've seen you with him, love. Jason, isn't he called?

How d'you know about him?

I'm not daft love. I've seen you with him hand in hand, and…

Dad!

… and the odd kiss now and then. And what Jake has said.

Jake! The little creep! Wait till I see him.

Jake has not done anything wrong love. It's just normal for kids to talk about each other. And you've not done anything wrong either. I'm glad for you.

Oh… so, er, what about this Farida then. Who is she?

I think you'd like her, love. She's from Iraq, and…

From Iraq! How come you've got in with a foreign woman?

Got in with? What's that supposed to mean?

You know, like, got in with, got a girlfriend I suppose!

You suppose right love. But girlfriend, boyfriend, at our age, it's sort of, not the right sort of words, if you know what I mean.

What do *you* call her then?

She's my – friend, sort of like, my best friend.

What about Charlie, and all your other mates? I thought

they were your best friends.

Yeah, we all have good mates, but it's not the same. You see, you can have good pals but still be lonely. It's a different sort of friendship. More like a need, if you see what I mean.

No. I don't know what you mean.

Well, you're only twelve, love. But you already have someone, a boy, who is your best mate, because, I don't know, maybe because your friends are getting boyfriends, and you didn't want to be left behind? Or maybe you felt like you needed a boyfriend, I dunno. What do you think?

How do you know what I need?

Because we've all been twelve years old, love, and we know how it felt. It's not just you. And we all have to start to learn how to do things, like kissing, maybe, to get a bit of practice for later on, sort of thing.

What do you mean, for later on?

For when you grow up of course. You don't just suddenly grow up and get married. It's usually after a few years of – of practice.

Practising what. You mean like – sex?

Yes. That'll come, sooner or later. And you'll probably want to keep it a secret. And that's ok. That's normal.

So, this woman you've been keeping a secret – have you been practising with her?

If you want to put it like that – yes.

Jesus! You're a dark horse aren't you. When were you gonna tell us?

I've just told you, haven't I.

Does Mum know?

I don't think so. Why?

Well… well… didn't she ought to know?

She would find out soon enough, I'm sure. There's a time and a place for everything.

Are you gonna tell her?

Not yet.

When?

I don't know. Maybe you could help?

You want me to tell her?

Would you like to?

I dunno. I'll have to think about it.

No rush, love. Let's keep things nice and steady for now. How do you think she would react?

Do you really want to know?

I can guess. But are we talking about her reaction. Or are we talking about yours? I can tell you're a bit upset.

Well… it's you keeping it a secret all this time, innit.

You mean like you and your boyfriend… ?

Oooh you!

You what?

You – whatever! I dunno what to say.

You could say – 'Oh, good for you Dad, I'm glad you've found a new friend.'

Yeah. I suppose so.

Think about it, love. It's a new thing to get your head round. But its life. No-one wants to be on their own for ever.

Yeah. So, will we get to meet her then?

Farida? When would you like to?

Mum?

Yes love?

Guess where we went last week.

To the pictures?

No.

Out for a meal?

Yeah. Sort of.

What do you mean, sort of?

Well, it wasn't Macdonald's.

Oh. I know you like Macdonald's. Did you have a picnic?

Sort of…

A sort of picnic. How many sorts are there?

This was at someone's house.

Do I know this someone?

I dunno. Three guesses.

Er… Mary Berry?

Don't be daft!

A friend of yours?

Getting warmer!

A friend of your dad's.

Yaay!

Now let me see… There's Charlie,

Naaaah!

And Greg…

Naaaah!

Oh, I know… It was Farida, wasn't it.

How d'you know about her?

A little bird told me?

You mean Jake? I'll kill him!

No. You don't have to do that. I need him. It was another

little bird. Birds get everywhere you know.

How'd you know about Farida then?

I've known about her quite some time. Your Dad used to do stuff with asylum seekers didn't he. He used to talk about her a lot.

What'd he say, then?

Just that he rather liked her, she was fun to be with, sort of thing.

Was this before you and him split up?

Not long before.

Was she the reason why you split up?

No, love. There was a lot more to it than that.

Did you know that him and her are, er…

In a relationship?

Yeah. You knew that already?

No. But I'm not surprised. I'm glad for him.

You're glad for him?

Yes. Why not?

You… you grown-ups, you…

Struggling for words are we Jodie?

You have a lot of secrets don't you!

Like you and your boyfriend, you mean?

Mum!!

I'm glad for you too Jodie. Life goes on doesn't it. Now here are you moving on into adult life, already. I was sixteen before I had my first boyfriend.

Wow! That's ancient!

What's she like then, this Farida?

She's er, quite nice.

Quite nice is she. How nice? How old?

She's very pretty. Probably about thirty, I dunno.

Mmmm. Prettier than me I bet!

Mum! You're all right.

Well, you look in a mirror love. That's how I looked when I was your age. And you're pretty too.

She's got two boys, seven and ten.

Did you meet them?

Yeah, but they mostly played with Jake.

What did you have to eat then? Did you like it?

Well, she started off by giving us all a load of sweets and cakes.

Ooooh dear!

Then it was, like, a ton of rice.

Ooooh dear!

And chicken, and funny sort of vegetables all covered in, er…

Spicy, was it?

Yeah. How d'you know?

Another of my little secrets love.

Did you like it?

I had to leave a lot of it, there was just too much.

But did you like it?

Yeah. Actually. Yeah. It was good. She was very smiley, really kind, she made you feel sort of…

Welcome?

Yes.

Will you go again?

Dad said they might come to our house next.

Is that ok with you?

I suppose so. It'll be someone else for Jake to play with.

Good.
You don't mind then?
Will *you* mind, Mum?
Why should I mind love? Your dad's got a right to have a life of his own, like you.
Yeah. I suppose so.

Dad?
Yes Jake?
Can we go there again?
You mean Farida's house?
Yeah. I like Sultan and Fa…
Fazil?
Yeah. It was cool.
You spent most of your time in their room. What were you up to?
They got some good computer games.
Maybe you can share some of yours next time?
Yeah. Cool.
What about the food?
All that rice! Didn't like it. Chicken were all right.
And what else?
Phew! All them sweets!
Aaah. That's why you like it, eh?
Yeah. Whatever.
Would you like them to come here?
Can we? Great!

Dad?
Jodie?

You know when we go to Mum's…

Yes.

She has a friend. She's there a lot when we go lately.

Oh yes. What's she called?

Marie, I think.

Is she nice?

Yeah. A bit quiet, but…

You get on all right?

Yeah. Why?

Good.

What do you mean – good?

You remember when we talked about feeling lonely?

Yeah.

Well, your Mum was lonely, even when we were together.

So, why did you split up?

Because… Because your Mum met Marie a few years before, and they sort of…

Sort of what?

It was like they both knew they were in the wrong kind of relationship.

Was Marie married as well?

Yes.

With kids.

Yes.

And what happened to her husband?

He left for another woman. The kids were a lot older than you and Jake.

Where are they now then?

Grown up and moved away. One's in uni, I think.

So, this house where Mum lives now…

Is Marie's, yes.

You mean they're like a…

A couple, yes.

A same sex couple?

It takes all sorts Jodie. We both knew that something wasn't right between us.

But you had children… I thought

What, that gay people don't want children?

Well, I…

People are all just human beings Jodie. Most of us can have children. Most of us do what they think is the right thing at the time, like everyone else. But sometimes you don't find out who you really are until a lot later.

So, our mum is, like, gay?

Your mum is a lovely human being Jodie, like you.

Am I dad?

Bit of a monster sometimes, but, you know, I love you. Your mum loves you too.

Its gonna feel different now when we go there.

Does your Mum treat you any different than she always did?

No. But…

But what, Jodie?

You mean Mum and Marie, they sleep together?

Yes. They love each other. I'm happy for her. You should be too.

And you and Farida…?

Yes love. We're happy too.

You want her to live here?

Yes love. It'll be a squash, but maybe one day we can find a bigger house.

When's this gonna happen then?

When the time is right darling. Not just yet. You need to get to know each other first.

She's a better cook than you!

Gee Thanks!

Tools in the van

Safia looks perplexed.

'She was knocking on that wall for a whole hour. I'm sure it was because of my kids. I didn't know what to tell them.'

George has heard this story many times before.

'Why do you say it was because of the children?'

'Well, she always does it when they are here. But kids are kids, aren't they. They're not angels. But you can't keep them quiet all the time.'

'How often are they here?'

'Well, my ex brings them three or four days a week. They stay with him three nights, you see. That's when I get most of my studying done.'

'You are a student?'

'Yeah. I work during the day and study at night. Accountancy.'

'So, you must be pretty busy, what with that and the children too.'

'I am. And I'm not too well either. I have a liver problem. She wouldn't know that.'

'You mean your neighbour?'

'She makes me feel worse.'

George knows that neighbours often play the health card in mediation. Safia looks and behaves likes a vigorous healthy young woman with fluent English, probably from a Pakistani background.

'So, you've mentioned the knocking. Was there anything else?'

'Oh yes! That was just the start of it. Soon as I came here, she started.'

'Started what?'

'The aggression. It's how I park me car, where my ex puts his van, where I put the bins. I can't do anything right.'

'What do you mean by aggression?'

'Well, she uses her bins to block my access to my parking space. And I'm not a confident driver. Especially reversing in a small space. I have to get out to move the bins so I can get my car in. She doesn't like that.'

'You said your ex parks there as well?'

'He has a van. He can't park it on the main road because of yellow lines, and there is nowhere else near enough. He's had his tools stolen from the van twice before.'

'He leaves his tools in the van?'

'Yes. He comes here about nine when he drops the children off and it would take too long to get all the tools out and put them back again.'

'Is there room at the back for a van?'

'Not much. But most people on here have visitors and they squeeze their cars in somehow. But she doesn't like it.'

'Have you spoken to your neighbour about all this?'

George already knows the answer.

'Yes, but she just shouts at me. You can't have a proper conversation with her.'

'What about your partner? What's his name?'

'Paul. He's tried as well but gets the same result. And she shouts at the children as well if they play in the garden.'

'How old are they?'

'Seven and twelve. I daren't let them out when she's around, because she frightens them.'

After some talk about carpeting and insulation and landlords George sums up and tells Safia he will speak to her neighbour and hope to arrange a meeting between them. He goes away thinking – tenant versus owner? Old versus young? Racism? Mixed race children? Who is this frightful old dragon next door?

*

He is surprised on meeting the dragon, when she turns out to be younger than Safia, a very friendly attractive blonde woman.

'Hi. I'm Geraldine. Come on in. Would you like a cuppa?'

George often would like a cuppa, but declines in the interest of neutrality, and a weak bladder. (which he doesn't mention)

'It's the noise, you see, the constant banging.' After a few prelims Geraldine begins the tale of torture she has to endure from the family next door.

'When her partner comes round, he bangs on the wall as

he goes upstairs'

'Why do you think he does that?' asks George, innocently.

'God knows,' she says, 'he's not a very nice man. We have words over the fence sometimes'

'What sort of words?' George thinks he can guess.

'Well, he's bumped my car more than once, and broke my wing mirror.'

'Did you see him do that?'

'No. But I know it was him. He's that sort of bloke. Vengeful. Know what I mean?'

'Why would he be vengeful?'

'Because… because I sometimes have to speak to her and her children about noise.'

'Tell me about the noise.'

'It's the kids running around and shouting, and her banging doors and stuff. And he's much worse. He slams the door when he comes in, and gets the kids all excited. I can hear them all going up and down the stairs and laughing.'

'Tell me a bit more about the cars. Did you say yours gets bumped?'

'You see everyone on here has their own space, and they mostly stick to it.'

'Do you all have the same size of space?'

'Yeah, but I have two spaces.'

'Oh. Why is that?'

'Because that's how it was when I bought the house. So, me and my partner have a car each, and when he's here that's where he parks.'

'But aren't the houses all the same width?

'Yes, but because of the turn in the road at this point, my house got two spaces.'

'Are there any written plans of the layout?'

'Not exactly. But the landlord of next door was going to try to clarify that. The two gardens are not exactly the same size either, and he was not clear where the boundary lay. So, I put my bins where I think the boundary should be.'

'Do all the neighbours put their bins on the road then?'

'No because they are not in dispute with their neighbours, are they.'

'Aha!' thinks George. Bin wars.

'It's her partner and his big van. He thinks he has the right to park it there whenever he comes round. So, I can't get my car out or in.'

'What, even though you have two spaces?'

'Yes. He's so inconsiderate. And rude!'

'Have you spoken to him about this?'

'You can't talk to him! He just shouts and doesn't listen.'

'Talking about the layout,' George decides to try a new tack. 'Does the road outside your houses belong to each of you?'

'No. It's not on the deeds.'

'So, is it a public road?'

'No. Its private. It doesn't belong to the council.'

'Who does it belong to then?'

'Nobody.'

'Nobody. Are the parking spaces marked?'

'No.'

'But you said your house has two spaces…'

'That's right. It does.'

George struggles to envisage one house having two spaces when all the houses in the terrace are exactly the same width. He decides to leave it.

'What would you like the outcome of this mediation to be?'

'I'd like her and him to stop banging and us to get on more like decent neighbours instead of him shouting at me. He isn't even a neighbour after all.'

Within the rules of mediation George is not allowed to pass on any information from one neighbour to the other. So, the fact that both of them are complaining about the same phenomenon remains in his note book.

Despite the strong language Geraldine has remained calm and pleasant throughout this conversation. George is left wondering what is really going on. Do we have a villain here?

Is it the house itself, which is often the elephant in the corner? Is it the age-old unspoken prejudice of class or race? This one can only be sorted out round a table. He decides to ask Safia whether her partner can come, but she says no. He refrains from asking her why she can say that without asking him, but makes a mental note of this. He also contacts her landlord, who agrees to come.

*

He agrees to come a little early so that George can grill him without the presence of the two antagonists. They are in a nearby community centre of some vintage. Arthur the landlord is of an even older vintage. Safia's house is the only one of his in this street. He has spoken to both of the women, and says he gets on fine with them. He can only speak for the needs of Safia, but it seems to George that there are some unwritten codes of behaviour on this back road, and Arthur is trying not to say what they are.

The code of behaviour for mediation however is written on laminated cards which sit before the two women when they arrive. Safia comes a few minutes before the start time and they make small talk until Geraldine arrives. George asks them to read the cards. He also tells them what the cards say, so as to avoid any difficulty with non-readers. Basically, no shouting, listen, don't interrupt. Quite unlike normal human behaviour.

And unlike normal humans they do stick to the rules. Safia gets first shot. She manages to list a number of grievances in a calm and orderly way rather like a manager at a team meeting setting out the agenda. Geraldine also sits quietly, with only a slight twitching of the mouth and flashing of the eyes, which George observes with faint amusement.

New and hitherto unmentioned items on Safia's agenda include the spreading of the contents of her dustbin all over her garden, and the placing of breeze blocks between the parking spaces, which she clearly implies must have been done by Geraldine. And she of course denies having any knowledge of bumped cars or broken mirrors. She lays it on a bit thick about her health problems, which are, she says, exacerbated by the aggression of her neighbour. And she makes a plea for understanding about the difficulties of bringing up adolescent children.

Geraldine in her turn, also manages to lay down a few home truths like punches from velvet gloves. She talks of the cost of car repairs and replacement mirrors, and the inconsiderate parking from someone who doesn't even live there.

George sees the restraint and formality being exercised by the women, who are both quietly seething underneath, and decides to divert attention towards Arthur.

'Do your tenants have a tenancy agreement Arthur?'

'Yes, why?'

'Do you have one with you?'

'No, sorry.'

'Does it say anything about parking spaces?'

'No. It's a private road, so that wouldn't apply.'

'As far as you know, do all the neighbours on that street have a designated parking space?'

'Yes, they do, I think.'

'Would that be one each?'

'That's right.'

George looks at Geraldine, who says nothing.

'Does the property of each house extend into the back street?'

'No, it's a matter of common law I think you'll find, that each one claims the right to that bit in front of their house for parking.'

'So, what about visitors? Can they park there as well?'

Geraldine speaks up here. 'As long as I've lived there, we all have family members visiting, and they somehow manage to squeeze a car in if they can.'

'Do you?'

'My partner comes to visit, yes.'

'And he parks there in your *double* space?'

'Yes.'

'So, what happens when Safia's partner comes?'

'Well, he has a van, and it's too big, and me and a few other neighbours can't get past it.'

'Arthur, would you like to comment on that?'

Arthur looks uncomfortably from one woman to the other.

'Well, if Safia's already parked in her space there isn't really room for anyone else, is there. If it were me, I would park it somewhere else.'

'Safia?' George looks at her expectantly.

'Well, it's like I said to you, he's had his tools stolen from the van twice before.'

'Why doesn't he take them out then?' Geraldine casts an incredulous look in George's direction and raises her eyebrows.

George looks at Arthur. 'I believe you might have something to say about this, Arthur?'

'Yeah, I was a joiner myself, and I always took my tools out of the van at night.'

'Safia?' George is playing table tennis doubles.

She looks frustrated. 'He doesn't have time to do that, he comes in so late most nights. And if he parked it else-where he would have to take more time to park it, bring it back and load up again.'

'Isn't that what most tradesmen have to do?' Geraldine lays it down with a hint of sarcasm.

George doesn't want to let this get out of hand.

'Tell us about the building blocks Geraldine.'

'My building materials, you mean. I am planning to reinforce my boundary, when Arthur tells us where it is. She keeps moving them.' Casting a baleful stare at Safia.

'What is this about the boundary, Arthur? Is there a plan on the deeds?'

'Not exactly' says Arthur, looking a bit uncomfortable.

'Sorry, I'm a bit confused here, Arthur, what do you mean?'

'Well, when these houses were built, they weren't all built at the same time, or by the same builders. Some of them have plans and some don't.'

'And is yours one with a plan or not?'

'No, it's not.'

'How could you find out about that?'

'I suppose I'd have to go to the council.'

'Could you do that, Arthur?'

'Well, I, um…'

'I think it would help Safia and Geraldine to know exactly which bit is which, don't you think?'

'Yeah, I suppose it would' he says, with a sigh.

'Geraldine, could you tell us about your relationship with Safia's partner Paul?'

'Paul, is that his name? It's nice to be told' she says acidly. 'it's not a relationship. It's more like a battle. He just shouts at me over the fence whenever he sees me. So, I shout back.'

'What do you shout about?'

'It's like he owns the place. And he's not even a tenant.

It's about cars and bins and kids, you know, all the stuff we've been talking about.'

By now Geraldine is losing her cool somewhat, and George needs to calm things down.

'Safia, have you talked to Paul about this? Why does he talk to Geraldine and not yourself?'

'Because I'm too scared to talk to her, that's why. I can't do with all this hassle. I'm trying not to upset her, but with the kids and everything else it's hard.'

'So, what do you think you could both do about that?'

He looks appealingly at both women. There is a long pregnant pause. Trying not to state the obvious Geraldine tries a diversionary tactic.

'Me and Arthur we talked about insulation, didn't we Arthur.'

'Arthur?' George projects a questioning look at Arthur.

'Um… well, Safia's house has no carpet on the stairs.'

'Is that something you might be able to arrange?'

'Yeah, probably…' He looks uncomfortable. Then he goes on. 'You see when these houses were built, and bits were added on, some had an insulating wall between them and others not. And they sort of joined up the joists between floors…'

'You mean,' says George, 'that sounds from one house carry into the house next door via the joists?'

'Aye, that's it. And Safia's is one of those.'

'Is there nothing that can be done to improve that then?'

'I suppose a bit more carpeting and underlay might help.'

Arthur sounds very uninterested in this idea.

'Is that do-able, Arthur?'

Geraldine and Safia look expectantly at him. Arthur nods silently.

'When do you think that could be done?' George knows he is putting pressure on the old man, but persists anyway. Something, or someone has to give here.

'Erm... maybe by September.'

This is July.

'Would that be helpful do you think, Geraldine?'

'I suppose so,' she says with a sigh. George sees a woman near the end of her tether.

'Going back to my earlier question,' he goes on, 'is there anything that the two of you could do to improve your relationship?'

'Suppose...' Geraldine begins carefully. 'Suppose you couldn't ask your, er, Paul, to take his tools out of the van when he stays?'

'No.'

Safia seems to think this is a step too far, or maybe, thinks George, she is afraid of him too.

'But...' Safia looks down at the table. 'Maybe you and I... what if we were to have a chat now and then about stuff.'

Having heard what she said earlier about being afraid to talk to Geraldine, George realises she has just made a huge effort. He smiles at Geraldine, who suddenly appears to relax ever so slightly. She turns her body towards Safia, and says...

'Um... yeah, ok. Would you like me to come round, or will you...?'

'I – I'll knock on your door.' Safia says quietly. She is shaking inside, and almost tearful.

'That would be great,' says George warmly. 'So, what have we agreed? Let's see…'

Stuey's night out

'You're not really gonna make him go abseiling are you sir?' Kelly asked Mr White, the teacher who had caused her to shed her own fear that very afternoon.

'Why not, Kelly?'

Mr White tugged at the last strap on Stuey's wheelchair.

'Well... you know... he's er... you know what I mean sir.' She didn't want to say out loud what was obvious.

'You mean he's just as scared as you were, Kelly?' Mr White knew something that she didn't know he knew.

'Ah, come one sir. How's he gonna do it?'

'Well,' he said with an enormous wink. 'Just you wait and see Kelly.'

So, they set off in the van with Stuey, Mr White, Miss Rankin, two more teachers and five children who were hand-picked from the day's activities. It was a beautiful mellow evening, and most of the camp were exhausted after a day of canoeing, hiking, riding and climbing. There was a lot of joking in the van bout who did what, who got wet, who fell off, and some were trying to wind up Stuey about tonight's episode.

'They've got a crane at top o't cliff, Stuey, what they've hired from Henry Boot. All you have to do is sit back and they'll wheel you up the cliff. Make sure you've got your seat belt on!'

Stuey had very little speech. He could only groan and grin at their humour. He had never seen a cliff, and had no idea what he was in for. So, it was not fear, but excitement that made his eyes shine, as his little body was thrown this way and that by the motion of the van on this rough terrain.

But not for long. Soon they were off the track and turning into a wooded path that became a large open space, surrounded on three sides by walls of rock. They all piled out, and Stuey was lowered on the hoist.

Everyone carried some piece of equipment, and they disappeared on the slope opposite, that rose a few feet and then went round behind the rock face. Stuey remained with Mr White and Miss Rankin, and he gazed up at the walls.

'Aaaaaaw!' he said. The smile had left his face.

'This is where we've been today, Stuey. Everyone has had a go at climbing up these walls, and abseiling down again.'

'Oh no!' thought Stuey. 'I don't believe it. He can't be serious!'

What came out was a little moan of fear, which Mr White seemed to recognise.

'We're going to get set up at the top there, and some of us are coming down the cliff, so that you can watch. Miss Rankin will stay here with you.'

'Phew!' thought Stuey. 'That's all right then!'

It was not long before the first girl appeared at the top of the cliff. She was standing on the edge with her back to him, holding on to a rope, which was being held tight by someone Stuey could not see.

'What's holding her up?' he thought.

His querulous cry was picked up by Miss Rankin.

'It's ok Stuey. The rope is tied to a big rock, and Mr White is paying it out. If he slipped, or if she lost hold of it, the rock would hold her, and the rope would just lock itself tight.'

In no time at all, Jade, the girl on the rope, walked backwards down the cliff, and calmly unstrapped herself, and came over to him grinning.

'See! S'easy!' she boasted, she who had only done it for the first time a few hours ago. Three more followed her, and they all made it look as if they were strolling down a school corridor.

'OK Miss Rankin!' the voice of Mr White from above, echoing stonily round the quarry.

'Your turn, Stuey!'

'Aaaaaaw!'

She and the last boy to come down began to push his chair across the quarry floor and up the grassy slope. Stuey's excited eyes took in the rock walls, the scree at the bottom, and the tops of the trees round the outside. His perspective changed when the party at the top came in sight, and he was delighted by the elevated view stretching back to the lake.

'Now you've seen it done Stuey, are you ready to have a go?'

Mr White kneeled down in front of him, a broad smile wrinkling his suntanned face. The rest of them stood looking at him expectantly. They were calm and glowing with good will.

'Yeah, Stuey, you can do it!'

Stuey turned his face to the cliff edge. Now he could not see the bottom. He looked at the big rock, around which the rope curved. He looked at the straps and metal clips on Mr White's body. He saw the eagerness in the other children's faces. He nodded and grinned. They all cheered.

Stuey was able to take a few steps at school. His lower legs were in callipers, and it was painful to walk very far. Mr White had calculated a way in which it would be possible for him to get down this cliff

'This is the belay,' he said, pointing to the big rock. The rope was tied round it. 'And this is the Carabina. This here is the Descendeur, and here…' reaching around Stuey's waist, 'this is the harness.'

He showed him how to pay out the rope through the carabina, and how to stop it.

'We're going to strap you behind Miss Rankin…'

'Woooo!' from some of the lads, grinning.

'And both of you will pay out the rope as you go down…'

'Aaaaaw!' Stuey's eyes widened.

He showed him how to pay out the rope.

'But even if you can't manage it, she will do it anyway, so you can't fall. Can he Miss Rankin?'

'I won't let you fall Stuey.'

'And I'll be strapped to the belay, and Mr Smith will be down below, waiting to meet you. OK?'

'Nnnnnn'

They took this to mean yes.

Then they stood him up to strap him into the harness. They tugged at the ropes and snapped the carabinas so as to make him feel secure. They linked him to Miss Rankin. The two of them stood with their backs to the cliff. Mr White started to release the rope.

'Oooh dear!' thought Stuey.

'Ooooh hell!' thought Stuey. 'I can't do it.'

'Right Stuey. Keep your legs straight. Take one step backwards.' It was a very small step.

'Now the other leg.' Two more little steps and his feet were right on the edge of the rock.

'Lean back Stuey.'

He did so, his heart thumping, as his body began to angle slowly backwards, and his feet stayed on the edge.

'Keep straight Stuey, don't bend your middle. Don't move your feet.'

'Can't move me feet anyway,' Stuey shouted to himself.

He was like the big hand on the clock approaching ten past, and Miss Rankin was edging back towards him. The did it so slowly. He did not dare to move anything, least of all his eyes, which were fixed on the back of her head.

'You all right Stuey?'

'Am I heck!' he thought.

The little whimper which came out was passed on by Miss Rankin.

'He's fine.'

'Now this is it. Don't bend your legs. Take one small step down.'

Stuey was now horizontal. Nobody could move unless he did.

'Don't want to move,' he thought. 'Can't move.'

But if he did'nt they would have to haul him up again.

'Ooooh. My knees hurt.'

He lifted a foot ever so slightly, concentrating hard. He placed it a few centimetres below the other.

'Good boy! Now the other! When you're ready.'

The other foot slid gently down to meet its mate.

'Good! Can you keep going Stuey?'

'Nooo!'

'Good!'

Mr White was braced against a small rock in front of him, leaning well back, his brown arms showing every vein and sinew.

Stuey knew he was utterly dependent on these people. He could not escape. All he could do was what he was told.

'Oooh, my aching legs!' he wished he could tell them.

After a few more steps he was sweating, not with fear, but with effort. It got to the point where Miss Rankin was also stuck out horizontally right above him. He noticed she too was taut in every limb. She said nothing. She was concentrating so hard. The other children were completely enthralled, and lay on their tummies watching him over the cliff edge. Only the voice of Mr White, calm and confident and the disinterested and very beautiful song of the evening blackbird nearby, coloured the still air.

'Mr Edwards, would you go down now please? Stuey –

are you alright?'

'Gotta keep legs on wall. Gotta keep legs...' His face screwed up in a frown.

There was no reply. Stuey was so absorbed in keeping his legs against the wall. He had never had to rely on them like this before, and he was not sure if he could take another step.

'Stuey?' Miss Rankin now.

'Uuuuuh!'

There was a groan from below, as Stuey tried one more agonising step. This time he lost it. His knees would no longer obey him. They buckled.

'Stuey!' Cries from the children.

Miss Rankin felt a violent change in her equilibrium, as Stuey swung towards the cliff face and out again, his legs now dangling loosely, as he hung in the harness like a child at the fun fair. His weight was shared between the two adults and the belay rock.

'Aaaaah, that's lovely!' thought Stuey.

The sudden break in the steady descent broke everyone's concentration. Down below Mr Edwards' hand went into his mouth. Miss Rankin was white with fear, but she managed to keep silent. Mr White faltered only briefly, as he was jerked forward by the sudden fall. But he then stood as he was before, and when the children calmed down, he went on talking to Stuey.

'Stuey! I know you're all right. Because I made sure you would be whatever happened. Don't go walking off now will you, 'cos I'm just gonna keep lowering you down until you reach the bottom. Mr Edwards is there with your chair. Just relax now. We'll do all the work.'

'Aaah. That's better!' thought Stuey.

He was not in control. Now that his legs had gone the pain had stopped. He was swinging about under Miss Rankin, and able to take a look around. A big grin appeared as he noticed the faces peeping over the cliff.

'This is much easier than the first bit,' he thought. Why couldn't they do this to start with?'

Slowly, so slowly, Miss Rankin walked down the cliff face. She was so tired now. Just as she felt she could no longer take another step, there was a joyful cry from below, a sort of 'Weeeeaaayy!' as Stuey realized he was down and about to be gathered up by Mr Edwards. There was a wild cheer and applause from above. He was lowered gently onto his bottom.

As he was helped into his wheelchair, Miss Rankin finished her descent, unclipped herself, rolled onto her back and lay with her eyes closed for several minutes. Even Mr White above, now sat with his back against the rock, eyes closed, and asked if anyone had brought a drink.

There was more hilarity on the way back.

'He's walking in the air,' they sang.

'Dinna dinna dinna dinna Batman!'

Stuey's face was joyful as he sang along with them in his tuneless groan.

'I'm gonna tell your mum I saw you hanging about them cliffs Stuey. 'Who was he hangin' about with, she'll say. What you gonna tell her?'

Stuey chortled.

They all felt something that words could not express. It

was noticed by the rest of the camp when they arrived, all as high as kites. Mr White was very quiet as he unpacked the gear, and went straight to his tent.

But Stuey grinned broadly at everyone. His mum would never believe it. As the story got round it grew in the telling.

He was a hero.

The witch and the gardener

'She's a compulsive liar, a big spender, an alcoholic, and is on anti-depressants. I don't wanna speak to her ever again!'

George the mediator is used to hearing these aggressive rants, often the result of pent-up anger and frustration, which tumbles out at the first opportunity when someone thinks they have found a sympathetic listener. It is a useful tactic to let them spill it all out in the first few minutes, while he maintains his usual impassive and imperturbable face, waiting for the steam to cool down.

The contrast between this and the mild-mannered professional missive from a social worker strikes him as ironic and faintly amusing. All par for the course.

'There's been a lot of tension/arguments around the divorce and issues with contact with the children so I feel by them attending the mediation it may help with them moving forward positively. Please could you confirm if this would be possible?'

'Of course, it will be darling,' George does not say, but sends his usual formal schedule of proposed dates and phone calls. A new slant on all of it is the lockdown situation, which means he has to meet all his clients on a screen, and hope that they have something a little more practical than just a mobile phone. It also means he can stay in bed a bit longer and not have to leave the house.

The first rant is part of the first call, when George is only trying to arrange a longer conversation. It must be something about my voice, he thinks. Trust seems to ooze out of them within the first few minutes. He has difficulty in getting the man to shut up, but after a few days his face is on George's screen. Michael seems to be sitting on the floor in his lounge with his tablet propped up somewhere near his feet, so that as the talk wears on his face gradually slips further down the screen until George has to ask him to prop it up again. It also gives him a view of the décor in Michael's room, which speaks of wealth. Not just wallpaper but a clever flower pattern which resembles a curtain of many coloured blossoms. Somehow this does not give the impression of the sort of place that would be occupied by a middle-aged man with close cropped hair and a furrowed brow and angry face.

'Yesterday,' he says, 'another step along the way – the divorce finally came through. Thank god for that.

'How long were you together?' asks George.

'Ooh, about five years, I think. But it was over long before that.'

'Meaning?'

'Meaning I started regretting it after about three years.'

'Why was that?'

'Well, she's such a bloody big spender. Money slips

through her hands like water. And I were stupid enough to keep giving it to her.'

'You must have loved her a lot then.' George looks for the positives.

'She were a very attractive woman, I have to admit – still is. Though that's not how I see her now, like.'

'How do you see her now, Michael?'

'She's a bloody witch, ain't she! Casts a spell over men like me, and I were stupid enough to fall for it.'

'But it didn't just end there, I think you were telling me on the phone?'

'No, I were paying her mortgage for seven months after we split up.'

'Is that over now then?'

'Aye, and I signed over the house to her as well, a four-bedroom semi.'

Hmmm, thinks George. 'Was that voluntarily?'

'Well… It were arranged by her solicitor. I couldn't afford one – I represent myself.'

Not very well thinks George, by the sound of it. 'What about children, Michael?'

'We have two little 'uns, four and five'.

'And one other, I think you said?'

'Aye, she's fifteen.'

'Is she from a former relationship?'

'Yeah, but she lives with me mostly, and with her Mum two days a week.'

'What about the little ones?'

'We share 'em. I have 'em three nights a week.'

'Nights only?'

'No. They are with me every other weekend.'

'Sounds like Natasha has them most then, is that right?'

'Well, her mother has 'em one night, and her sister another.'

Complicated, thinks George.

Michael goes on, 'and, er, I see 'em sometimes when I'm doin' 'er garden.'

'Doing her garden?'

'Well, she wanted it to be safe for the kiddies, so I were putting up fences and shrubs, you know.'

'Are you still doing her garden?'

'Well, I were until last month.'

'Have you finished now then?'

'Well, she's got a new fella, hasn't she.'

'But you said you split up two years ago.'

'And there were these abusive texts from her mum'

'Abusive texts? What was that about?'

'Well, I suppose it was because I stopped paying her maintenance'

'Hang on, says George,' you said you paid off her mortgage, paid over the house, paid the council tax, share the child care, and you were paying maintenance. Is Natasha working?'

'She is now. But she were studying to be a nurse.'

'She works as a nurse. Full time?'

'Yeah.'

George takes a minute to think. 'And are you working?'

'I work from home. Self-employed.'

'Sounds like quite a complicated life you both lead. Where you live now – do you own the house?'

'I do. Why?'

'Oh, I'm just trying to figure out the logistics and the financial side of things. And, er… I'm a little puzzled as to why you kept on doing the garden so long after you split up.'

In all this time Michael has maintained a serious and determined attitude, un smiling and forceful. George thinks there must be more to this than meets the eye.

'I love my kids you know.'

'Yes, I'm sure you must do. What about the older daughter? Does she get on with the little ones?'

'She does. But not with my ex.'

'Why is that then?'

'Well, it's like, you know, teenagers and dads and new relationships… it's hard for her. And there was an incident with Natasha…'

'An incident?'

'She tried to strangle her.'

'She tried to strangle her?'

'They had a fight like.'

'Over what?'

'I dunno, just two women fratching, you know how it is.'

Do I? Thinks George. So. The mother, the ex and the older daughter. What is going on, I wonder. George thinks he has enough to get on with, and winds up by saying he would speak to Natasha soon, and that if she is willing, he would try to arrange a meeting of the three of them soon. Michael, surprisingly, goes along with this, despite what he said earlier. Trust the process, thinks George. Trust the process.

*

Three days later Natasha is on his screen. A lovely face, thinks George, well-groomed blonde hair, shoulder length, dangling ear rings, low cut dress, smiling. She looks as if she's ready for a night out. He starts by getting her to repeat the details of the child care arrangement. She is very precise on this, and it matches what Michael had told him earlier. With a few extras.

'I'm finding it really hard to manage it all, you know, the school uniforms, dinner money, and all that. And he's stopped paying maintenance now.'

'Was that part of the divorce agreement?'

'Well, no, because I got the house, and he had a £20K pay off. The maintenance was what he paid before all that, before I was working full time.'

'Forgive me', says George, 'but I'm not quite sure of the financial situation. Have I got this right? You got the house, no mortgage to pay, you're working full time, you share the child care. Michael also has a house which is paid for, he works full time. You both have a car. Is it a matter of the difference between your salaries?'

'Well yes, he earns at least twice as much as me. He's not exactly poverty struck, what with a new motor bike AND a BMW!'

So, they are both big spenders, think George, if Michael is to be believed.

'And I'll tell you something else. There are the nasty texts from his mother'

'Nasty texts? Can I ask what's that about?'

'Well, she keeps going on about me and the kids, how I'm neglecting them, and spending too much. And them having more fun with him than with me. Because he doesn't have to care for them all the time, they get taken out to Macdonald's, playing in the park, going to the pictures and all that sort of stuff. I don't have time or money to do all that'

'Is she part of the child care, as well as your mum?'

'Yeah, cos when he has them, he don't always look after them all the time. She has them sometimes as well.'

'So let me get this straight – the children are looked after by you, by Michael and by two grandmas.'

'And my sister as well, she picks them up from school one night and gives them their tea.'

'That's quite a lot of people.'

'Yeah. And sometimes they don't know who's picking them up.'

'Do they have different set of clothes at each house?'

'Yeah, but he's not so good at washing them and that sort of stuff. He brings them round here sometimes.'

Another form of dependency, thinks George. Two kids. Two grandmas. Two parents. One aunt. Two rich people.

'And ... you are in a new relationship I believe?'

'Yeah. Stephen.'

'Are you living together?'

'No. he's here two or three nights a week.'

'Does he do any child care?'

'No. he's got two of his own. From a previous marriage.'

'And is he involved in the same sort of arrangement with his ex?'

'Yeah. It's complicated!'

'Sounds like it,' says George, who is running out of questions about child care and relationships. Better stick to the matter of the moment, he thinks.

'This, er, mediation, was requested by your social worker.'

'Yeah.'

'Because...?'

'Because of the voluntary incident.'

'Voluntary incident?'

'When me and Michael's daughter sort of fell out?'

'Fell out over what?'

'Can't remember now, but it sort of got a bit physical.'

'Does that mean one of you got hurt?'

'And then he reported me to the social.'

'I see. So does that mean they think someone is at risk?'

'Suppose so.'

'But it's also about your relationship, isn't it?'

'Yeah. It needs sorting out.'

'What would you like to sort out?'

Natasha sighs. 'That's why you're here isn't it?'

'All right. I presume you would like something to change then.'

'Yep. I like to sort things out by talking. He doesn't want to talk. Keeps sending me little notes with the kids.'

'What sort of things?'

'About changing the days for child care.'

'I thought you had a fixed schedule for that.' 'We do. But he keeps wanting to mess it up.'

'How does that affect the children?'

'They get upset, and that upsets me, and it upsets my Mum and my sister.'

'I see. So, you would want to know where you are with that.'

'That's right. And then there's the maintenance.'

'You want to talk about money as well.'

'Yeah. So, I know where I am, and who pays for what.'

'We will put that on the agenda then. Anything else?'

'How we communicate.'

'You would like to talk. He wants to write. Why do you think that is?'

'He hates me, doesn't he.'

I'm not so sure about that, thinks George.

'We will put communication on the list. Is there anything about the grandparents you would like to discuss?'

'Well, they are both writing stupid texts to me and each other.'

George can't involve any extras on his cast list, unless one of them asks for it. This he sees as primarily about a broken love affair. They talk about a date for the joint meeting.

*

George has a reputation for bringing about agreements between warring parties that stretches back over more than twenty years. He was pleased that Michael had agreed to meet Natasha face to face, but online. It would be difficult, but not impossible. He has devised a set of conditions that both parties must agree to, and these are dispatched a few days ahead of the meeting. They include 'uninterrupted time.' This is when each party gets to speak without the other commenting. This is the hardest part for the other party to endure. It also includes a request for no judgmental or abusive remarks, and that extends to body language as well. He must assume that both parties know what this means. And thinking of his conversation with Michael, he has his doubts.

*

On the day, he begins by reminding them about confidentiality. Michael immediately jumps in.

'I want to know if there's anyone else in the room!'

Natasha is taken off guard, but gathers herself and turns her camera round so as to take in the whole of the room. There is no-one else there.

'How about your room, Michael?'

George feels he has to ensure equality.

'Course not! You don't think I would do that, do you?'

He turns his tablet round.

'Thank you. Natasha, would you begin please? Michael this is your turn to just listen, without commenting, OK?'

He asks her to repeat the list of points she was looking for. She begins to describe the arrangements for child care days and dropping off times. Michael butts in again.

'You don't need to tell us that. We already know what time to drop them off!'

'Michael – Could you please wait until Natasha has finished, like we agreed?'

'Yeah, but it's all right her saying that, but she needs to stick to the arrangement herself.'

'Yes, we will come to that in due course. Please let

Natasha finish, and I will come to you in a few minutes.'

Natasha continues. She talks about the anxiety felt by the two young children about drop off times and knowing who they will be with from one day to the next.

'You know damn well who they are gonna be with! It's written down, innit!'

'Michael, please, I will ask you again, please, just listen, and don't interrupt.'

Michael pulls a face, and turns away from his tablet. Natasha continues.

'The kids are only four and five. They are not as well organised as you are Michael. There are you and I, your Mum, my Mum and my sister all involved. At that age they don't even know what day it is, let alone who is collecting them.'

'Well, they seem to know what they're doing when they're with me!'

'Michael – I would like us to take a break for a minute. Natasha, if it's all right with you, I will mute you for a minute, while Michael and I have a little talk.'

George asks Michael if he remembers the guidelines that he had previously agreed to. Like a teacher, he asks him to repeat the relevant item about interrupting. Michael sullenly does so, and agrees to stop interrupting. Back together again, George asks Natasha to continue.

'And when they come to your house, there's never anyone at the door to greet them.'

'Is that so, Michael?'

Michael pulls a face of exasperation. 'No, it's not. Like I said before, she's a liar. I am always there when they arrive.

They can see me standing at the window.'

'Michael, we had an agreement about that word, it's very provocative. Natasha?'

Natasha ploughs on, becoming more and more unsteady in her voice.

'It's like I told you, George, he won't speak to me. He can't even come to the door just to say hello to the children.'

'And that's a point you would like an agreement about?'

Michael bursts in again. 'You want me to agree to stand at the door instead of the window?'

'Michael, it's a small point, but I think Natasha feels it's important to the children.'

George has abandoned the uninterrupted time rule, in favour of seeking one agreement at a time. Michael reluctantly agrees.

'BUT! – what about the time, eh? She's never on time, is she! If we say five o'clock it's more like gonna be half past or six o'clock! And I never know if it's her or her mother or her sister gonna be there.'

'Michael,' Natasha comes back.

'You work at home, all right. I work in a hospital. Things happen. People's lives are what I have to deal with. They don't work to a clock like you. I can't always get away in time.'

'And is that why', George butts in,' you can't always be certain about the time of arrival?'

'And there's traffic too, at that time of the day.'

'Michael?' Michael sighs and looks at his feet, but says nothing.

'Shall we move on and look at the next point?'

George wants to get it over. He wishes he had never started.

'It's the clothes,' Natasha begins.' He keeps on buying them things he thinks they need, and I buy the same stuff sometimes, and I'm on a tight budget.'

'Do you not talk about that beforehand Michael?'

'No. If I see there's something they need I just get it. Looking at the stuff she sends them in sometimes it's pretty obvious.'

'What's obvious, Michael?'

'That they're not being properly looked after. And it's not that she's short of money, or she wouldn't be able to buy all that booze she hasn't told you about, would she!'

At this point Natasha starts to sob.

'You're the one to talk about money! What about that damned motor bike you don't need, and who drives a bloody BMW, eh?'

George decides to call a halt. This is not what he is used to. He needs to take control, and only way to do that is to stop.

'Natasha, I think we need to take another break, and I need to talk to Michael again. Shall we say we re-join in about half an hour? You go and have a coffee.'

*

George knows that if they do not come to an agreement then things are likely to get much worse. The children are obviously suffering from the tension between the two adults. He decides to take a potentially career breaking risk.

'Michael. This is not going well is it.'

'No.' Michael is still as tense as a flagpole.

'When you agreed to come to a meeting I was impressed, because that was not what you said to start with.'

'No.'

'I thought it might just be possible to make a difference here, if you were willing to talk to Natasha. Am I right?'

'Yes.'

'But you're not talking are you. You're shouting. You are showing your anger.'

Michael says nothing, but his lips are pursed as he stares at the ground.

'Do you want things to get better, Michael?'

'Yes.'

'Do you love the children, Michael?'

'Course I bloody do.' Michael's voice is cracking.

'You told me you never wanted to speak to Natasha again. But that's not true, is it Michael.'

Michael nods.

'Do you hate her?'

He nods again.

'I don't believe you, Michael. You still love her, don't you.'

Michael's eyes begin to fill with tears, and he begins to sob.

'You love her a hell of a lot don't you.'

'I do. I still love her. I bloody do.'

'Yes. I thought so.'

George gives him a few minutes to settle down. Michael's body starts to unwind. His shoulders relax, he sighs and wipes his eyes.

'Do you think she knows you still love her?'

'I dunno. She doesn't bloody show me that.'

'Why do you think that is?'

'I dunno.'

'I think you do, Michael.'

'Tell me then, if you think you know so much.'

'It's because you are so angry at your loss, you feel you have to punish her that at every opportunity, am I right?'

Michael remains silent.

'Am I right Michael?'

'Yes.'

He starts to cry again.

'In fact, you have become a completely controlling angry bastard, but you have actually lost control of the situation, and you take it out on all and sundry.'

Michael cannot find the words to respond to this, and just sits with his head in his hands, like a prisoner waiting for his punishment.

'So shall we talk about what you have to do then?'

*

When the meeting resumes, George immediately feels in control again. He picks up where they left off, and to Natasha's complete surprise, Michael agrees to cooperate on all her points. He is quiet, and takes his time, and there is no aggression or criticism. He will stop writing officious little notes, and critical texts, and will pick up his phone and talk with her. He will try to persuade his mother to stay out of it. They will discuss what clothes the children need, and who will buy them.

Before the days of corona virus, George had been used to seeing the parties smile and shake hands, and often go away chatting amiably with each other. He misses those days. Just switching off the Zoom screen lacks dignity and humanity.

But just before they part, Michael asks to speak.

'Natasha love?'

Natasha looks surprised.

'Yes Michael?'

'I'm sorry love. I'm sorry.'

'I'm sorry too love. I really am.'

She smiles, with tears in her eyes once more

Leave me alone.

Colin is uncomfortable.
He stands near the desk of the housing office. There are two people talking to the officers behind the desk and he has to wait. He would prefer to be the only customer. He will have to say why he is here. It is eleven o'clock and he arrived precisely at eleven. Now it will be late because he has to wait. Being late increases his anxiety.

'Hello Colin.'

The woman who he met here before suddenly appears beside him. He had not noticed her sitting nearby as he was so focussed on his task. He can't remember her name. She smiles at him. He does not smile back. She explains that the little room where they will meet is occupied by someone else, and they are over running. His meeting will be late and he does not know how late. This makes him more anxious. He likes things to run as planned.

The man behind the desk goes to the door of the little room and asks if they will be long. He tells Colin it will be a few minutes. Colin stands there awkwardly, not knowing what to do. There are only three seats for waiting and he does not feel comfortable sitting next to the woman and the man. They might start to chat about nothing in particular, and chat is not part of his routine.

After five minutes the room is vacated and they enter. He sits in the same seat he sat in last time. The woman thanks him for coming. She reminds him of their names, George and Julie. She starts to remind him of what happened before. They visited Colin's neighbour and he was worried about coming to a meeting with Colin, so they are starting again. They have been to see Harold this morning and he was thinking again about a meeting. He might want to bring a friend for support.

'I don't want to meet any of those neighbours of his,' says Colin, 'they're the ones who are abusing me.'

Julie reminds him that he did agree to a meeting when they met before.

'You could bring someone to support you if you like,' she says with a smile.

'I don't know anyone,' says Colin.

George reaches into his bag and pulls out some papers. 'I've got some information here that I told you about before.'

He figures that Colin needs distracting. 'You said there was no support group for Asperger's here, but I found out there was. This lady here,' he points to a name on the document, 'she said she would come to see you if you want. And there's a group that meet every month that you could join.'

George notices too late that there is only an email address and a phone number on the document. Colin has no phone or computer, and will only accept letters by way of communication.

Colin is panicked by this new idea. He takes the papers from George and puts them into his bag without looking at them.

'Will you have a look at them later, Colin?'

'I don't want to meet anyone in Halifax. I don't feel as if I belong here. I go to Leeds every week, where I used to live. When you asked me to meet you at a bar, I didn't know what to do. I don't go to bars.'

'It wasn't a pub sort of bar, just a big open Cafe at the Square Chapel, Colin.'

'I don't like speaking to people in public places.' Colin is resisting with all his might.

Julie thinks she needs to change the subject before Colin walks out on them.

'If this meeting goes ahead, Colin, and we don't know yet if it will, where would you like to meet? We can't use this room, 'cos it's too small.'

'I don't like public places.'

'So, if we can get a room that's private enough, would you come?'

'I didn't like this place,' Colin continues. 'I'd never been here before.'

'I'm sure we can find somewhere where you will feel comfortable,' says Julie. And George and I will be there. We will make sure nothing goes wrong.'

'They won't listen,' Colin tries a new tack. 'They are not going to change anyway. What's the point?' He really can't bear the idea of sitting round a table with these terrible neighbours who are persecuting him.

George brings out an old tried and tested line. 'In every mediation we have ever done, I think every single person has said to us what you just said, Colin. But they are always wrong.' (He wishes he hadn't said that) And in every case they always feel better about it afterwards, and things do change for the better.'

'Do you really want things to go on like they are now, Colin?' says Julie.

'I just want them to leave me alone,' Colin says. 'I don't want to have to speak to them at all. I don't want them to look at me, or wait for me, or make those gestures.'

'Sometimes people agree not to speak at all,' George presses on. 'But they agree to not speak in a polite sort of way, if you know what I mean. You could just say hello, or good morning, or something like that.'

'I never say hello or good morning to anyone,' Colin blusters. 'I don't like having to speak to people I don't know.'

'Maybe that is part of the difficulty,' says George. 'Maybe they find that hard to deal with. Most people just say hello or good morning even to people they don't know. That's what normally happens.' ('Damn!' says George to himself.)

'Are you saying I'm not normal then?' Colin is deeply upset. This is the whole nub of the matter, the obscene gestures, the laughing at him, the staring, the blocking of his path.

Julie kicks George under the table.

'I don't think that's what George meant,' she says

sweetly. 'It's just that most people feel uncomfortable if someone they meet every day never says anything or looks at them. It hurts people's feelings. And that's what this meeting will be about. Both sides need to hear how the other feels about the present situation.'

'I don't want anyone knowing my feelings,' says Colin. 'That's a private matter'

'But it may help for them to know how you feel about the things they are doing to you. If you never talk about it they may decide for themselves who you are, and get the completely wrong idea. And you're obviously not happy about it are you Colin?'

'That's why I told the police and the council. I want it to stop.'

'And what happened, Colin, did they put a stop to it? Has anything changed?'

There is a long pause, as Colin fishes out some official documents. He knows nothing has changed, but he feels if he keeps it all in writing and official, he will be more comfortable with it. He won't have to be personally involved and actually have to talk to his neighbours. He pushes the documents towards Julie.

'Colin,' George returns to the fray. 'Can I tell you what upsets people the most? There are three things. One is Police. Secondly getting official letters through their door. Third thing is cameras.' Colin has been photographing his neighbours every time they pass him by, so he can show these films to the police.

'Can you tell me what they did about it after you showed these things to the police or the housing officer?'

'They spoke to the neighbours,' Colin says, without conviction.

'Did they actually do anything though? Has anything got better?'

'No.'

'Do you know why that is, Colin?'

'No.'

'It's because they are not trained in mediation. That is why they always refer you to us, because they know mediation usually makes things better.'

There is another pause. Colin shows no sign of any emotion, or willingness to go along with this. He is simply afraid of being made to come out of his comfort zone.

Julie senses that things are not moving forward.

'Colin,' she says quietly, 'We will try to get your neighbour to come to the meeting, either by himself or with a friend. Will you take a look at those names George gave you, as they are willing to support you. We will give you enough notice in writing, so you know what is happening next. So we will leave it for now, and hope to see you soon.'

*

Harold is uncomfortable.

These two people sitting in his little flat were here before. He thought he had got rid of them, but they have come back. They have come to talk again about that awkward nutter upstairs who he wishes would go away. Harold is not used to having long conversations with clever people. But they seem nice enough.

'Thanks for letting us come to see you again,' says Julie with great warmth. 'We've seen Colin again and he is still willing to meet you if you want to.'

'Who's Colin?' says Harold.

'You know, Mr. Robertson upstairs that you told us about, remember?'

'Oh, I didn't know his name like. 'Cos he never speaks you know.' Harold has moved an inch in Colin's direction, although he would not see it like that.

'Do you think he knows your name Harold?' Julie knows the answer, but is laying the ground for a humanisation of the situation.

'No, he wouldn't would he, 'cos we never get to talk,' says Harold, who has had an entirely different way of communicating with his neighbour.

'Do you get to see many of the people in these flats?' George asks, and he also knows the answer.

'No, we like to keep ourselves to ourselves, no-wat-a mean' says Harold with a little grin that shows several missing teeth. 'I just go out to me little job at the volunteer centre, and there's not many people about at that time o' day.'

'Yeah, but if you do see someone do you say hello to them, Harold?'

'Course I do,' says Harold, 'but 'im upstairs, ya know he never says owt. An' I sometimes hold door open for him, but he don't seem to like it. He just waits till I've gone and says nowt. Ah think 'e's a bit mental, no-wat-a-mean?' Harold smiles again assuming that they know what he means.

'So, you've never really talked to him about anything, have you Harold?' Julie has got the picture, but she wants to paint it a bit plainer for Harold to see a different angle. 'Do you know why he does that?'

'Nah. Din't 'e tell ya?'

Harold genuinely has not given it much thought, and is a bit worried about this couple probing his behaviour. George and Julie know that there is more to it than this. Something is going on here between neighbours which is causing enormous stress to Colin. But they cannot tell Harold what they know, only keep probing and probing until he comes up with something nearer the truth.

'Have you any friends here in the flats, Harold?' George asks, knowing that this little man, who looks as if butter wouldn't melt in his mouth, is part of a systematic campaign to belittle his neighbour upstairs.

'I do see a man who I talk to when we meet on't stairs,' says Harold cautiously. 'I see 'im nearly every day.'

'What's his name Harold, do you know?'

George is not surprised when Harold says he does not know the man's name. This block of flats is full of people who belong nowhere and to no-one. They keep themselves apart for reasons of their own.

'Would you say he was a friend then Harold?'

'Yeah, 'e's quite friendly, like,' says Harold.

'Do you know what flat he is in?'

'No, I've never been in anyone's flat. And no-one's ever been in mine either,' says Harold, who probably could barely make the cost of tea and biscuits for two.

Julie tries to move on another inch. 'You know you said last time we met that you didn't think you would want to meet Colin.'

'Colin?'

'Mr Robertson upstairs, the man we are talking about.'

'Oh no, I don't want to meet him.' Harold shakes his head and makes a gesture with his finger towards his head that means 'mental'.

'Do you think you could ask your friend that you mentioned if he would come to a meeting with you to support you?'

'Ooh, I don't know,' says Harold. This sounds like completely new territory for him to embark on. 'I don't know what flat 'e lives in'

'Do you think he might like to talk to us, Harold?'

This is a long shot, and Julie knows the answer is probably no. But neither party is giving an inch, so she thinks about chipping away at the edges of an insoluble unpalatable situation.

'How about, when you see him tomorrow, you tell him what we have been talking about, could you do that, do you think?'

'I might not see 'im tomorrow' Harold is looking shifty.

'Yeah, but if you do, what do you think? Julie smiles broadly.

'You do want things to change, don't you Harold?' George smiles broadly.

'Yeah, I suppose so,' says Harold, who rather enjoys having someone to tease in his empty life. But having to sit in a room with the bastard! God! What are they asking?

*

Colin has had a letter.

He doesn't have a mobile, and he can't afford a landline. Having any kind of phone means he would have to speak to people he couldn't see and didn't know. He would also have to speak in reply to whatever was said, with no time to think about his answer, and no warning of what they might say. And having no friends, Colin can see no reason to have a phone. It would be a waste of money.

Having a letter meant that he could sit and read it in his own time, and think about what to do. He could take his time in replying, and only when he felt sure of what he would say. This one had a name of someone in the housing office, so he might go to the phone box and call them, or he might go to the office and hope to see them. Either of these options filled him with dread.

But he had managed to fix an appointment, days in advance. And so here he is again, waiting at the desk in a different building to the one they met in before. That woman is here again. She comes over to greet him with a smile. The man is missing.

'George is with your neighbour, Colin. Harold has brought a friend to support him. But they will stay in another room. You and I we can go in this other room.'

She manages to shepherd him into a new room, empty but for a table and a few chairs, some water and some biscuits. Colin sits. He is feeling sick. Julie explains what will happen next.

The routine is that the two mediators will talk to each party in turn, and shuttle between rooms with messages from the other party, until some points of agreement are reached. What she doesn't say is that they hope to get them both in the same room after a while, but she knows this is a long shot.

George appears at the door. He introduces himself and Julie again, knowing that Colin will probably have forgotten again, as it was not written down. They thank him for coming, and acknowledge the effort he has made to be there.

'I don't want to talk to them, you know.' Colin puts on his suit of armour. It's not brightly polished. But it feels comfortable.

'We know, Colin,' says Julie, but what we want is for your views to be heard by your neighbour, and theirs to be heard by you, if that's all right.'

'Tell us again what it is that upsets you so much,' says George, who already knows the answer.

This time Colin has brought a list, in case he should forget anything. 1. Having to speak to people when we meet on the stairs. 2. People waiting to hold the door open for me. 3. People talking about me. 4. People making rude signs (he gestures)

'And what would you like to happen, Colin?' Julie also knows the answer, but it is important to get people to actually say it out loud.

'I just want them to leave me alone. I told you before.' Colin is very uptight, because he thinks these people should already know what he told them before, and the sense that his neighbours are just in a nearby room.

They thank him and ask him to wait while they visit the

people in the other room. Help yourself to a drink and biscuits, Colin'

*

They go through the same routine with Harold and his friend.

'Nice to meet your friend, Harold. 'And she thanks Michael the neighbour for coming with Harold. 'You're all right, love,' he says. 'No trouble.'

'That's good Michael.' They are laying on the courtesy a bit thick.

Julie asks Michael if he'd like to add anything of his own.

'Well, I'd say he's not right in the head, no-what-a mean. Not speakin' like, and taking photos with a camera every time he comes out o't door.'

'Why do you think he does that then?' Colin enquires.

'I dunno. Makes us feel fair uncomfortable though, when we're only trying to 'elp like.'

'What do you do to try and help, Michael?'

'Well, some of us have a bit of chat at bottom o't stairs when we meet, and if someone wants to get by we might hold door open for 'em. That's all.'

'Is that all, Michael?' Julie knows there is a bit more to it than that.

'Well sometimes 'e just stands there, not speakin', and 'e won't come by.'

'Do you know why that is?'

'Nah, d'you know Harold? 's not normal is it, like.'

Harold shakes his head.

'Would you like to know what Colin says about it?' George chooses what he hopes is the right moment. They tell the pair what Colin thinks about them.

'Well, I'll go to 't foot of our stairs!' breathes Michael, with an incredulous look at Harold. 'Sounds like a right bloody nutter, no-wat-a mean?'

'Have you ever said that to him Michael?' Julie goes for a little risk.

'Course not! What d'ya tek me for?'

'Are you sure there is not something you might have done that causes him to think like that?'

'Don't know what ya mean love,' Michael decides to bluff it out.

'It was something Colin said about certain gestures?' George ventures.

'Gestures?'

George risks making that gesture, with an enquiring look on his face.

'Harold,' says Julie, 'what do you reckon?'

Harold looks at Michael, and they both grin knowingly.

'Ah well,' says Michael, 'maybe I might have done summat like that at one time. But ya know its ony a bit o' fun, like.'

'But Colin thinks you mean it, Michael, and he's very upset about it,'

'Well, we're very upset about him tekkin' bloody photos!' Michael hits back.

'So now you know what upsets him,' says Julie, 'is it ok if we tell him what you said that gets you upset?'

So, they have got so far with both of them still in the

room, and decide to go for round two, in the next room.

When they get there Colin has gone missing.

*

George, not wanting to go through the whole rigmarole of writing letters and booking the room yet again, rushes outside and spots Colin walking briskly away from the building.

'Colin. Stop a minute.' He runs to catch up with him.

'I don't want to go through with it,' says Colin, 'I just want to get another flat somewhere else.'

'Listen Colin,' George manages to bring him to a halt. 'We've made a bit of progress in there. I'd like you to come back and hear what the others have said. Please. We know you don't want this to go on and on. But I think both you and your neighbours want things to get a bit better, don't you. I think we can help you with that. Come back in Colin.'

Colin stands in the busy street in some agony. He has pushed himself to his limit in coming this far against all his strongest instincts. And now he knows what he has always done, over and over again in his life. He has run away.

'Please don't run away again, Colin'.

George has just taken another enormous risk. Colin stands stock still. George stands in front of him, his arms gesturing towards the building they have just left, with a smile on his face.

'Colin?'

After an age of indecision, Colin turns, and silently walks back towards the building.

*

Julie is back in the other room with Harold and Michael when they return. She and George made an arrangement about what must happen next. George ushers Colin into the original room. George pours a drink for himself and Colin and offers some biscuits. He takes his time.

'Colin, they know how it makes you feel, when they stand around waiting, and make those gestures. And we asked them how it makes them feel when you don't talk to them, and when you take photos. I think we can say it's about the same on both sides. What would you say to that?'

Colin says nothing. The language of empathy is not in his repertoire.

'Do you remember what we said earlier about people not communicating? That in all mediations that is what it comes down to in the end. Now you have a choice. You can carry on just the same and nothing will get better. You can run away to another flat in another town, and not communicate with anyone there. The chances are you will get the same reaction from your new neighbours.'

'OR… you can make a start now, and just say hello to your neighbours in the next room. And then, I promise you, things will slowly start to get better.

Think about it.'

Colin thinks about it. He feels like a rat cornered by a

cat. He desperately wants to get up and leave. He is sick and afraid.

George waits, and munches his biscuit. After a while, since Colin is still there, he decides it is time to take the final risk.

'I'm going to open the door now, Colin, and they will just come in and sit down quietly. You just wait. It will be all right.'

He gets up slowly, smiles at Colin, and goes to the door of the next room and opens it a little, nodding to Julie on the other side.

The three of them enter quietly and sit round the table.

'Colin, this is Harold and his friend Michael, and Julie.'

'Hello Colin,' says Michael sheepishly. 'I'm sorry lad, I didn't know your name, like.'

And bravely he stands up and reaches across the table to shake Colin's hand. Colin does not know what to do, but George smiles at him and gestures for him to take Michael's hand. He does. A limp grip, but a first ever hand shake.

Harold does the same. Colin responds. He is lost for words.

George continues. 'Now you both know what it is that's been upsetting you both. Maybe one of you might like to say something? '

Michael looks at Harold, who shows no emotion, but slowly shakes his head. He has never in his life been in a situation like this before. Having few friends, and living alone, he has been shaken by this scenario where he has had to talk about his feelings to complete strangers. But he realises that Harold is not going to speak.

'Harold and me, like,' says Michael, 'we meet on't stairs nearly every day and say 'ello, ya know. And when you come by and say nowt its sort of upsettin' if ya know what I mean. An' dya know what? 'E's gonna come and ave a cuppa at my flat now and again, and that's what we've been talkin' about next door.'

It is the longest speech Michael has ever made all in one go, and he feels quite pleased with himself. He finally plucks up courage and looks at Colin.

'An' ah'm sorry lad. For upsettin' ya. It'll not 'appen again.'

'Ah'm sorry too Colin,' says Harold at last. This is the first thing he has ever said to Colin, and it feels like he was shrugging off a heavy overcoat.

'Colin?' George looks at him, and sees a frightened little boy, out of his depth. 'Anything to say, Colin?'

After a long pause, Colin whispers 'Thank you. I'm sorry too.' He has never in his life apologized to anyone. It is his first step in learning a new language. He sits awkwardly looking at the table.

'It would be nice if ya could just say hello, when we meet, or good mornin' or say summat, Colin, but not nothing.' Michael goes on. 'An' ya know we wouldn't mind if ya felt like having a cuppa wi' us from time to time, eh? What do ya say?'

Colin just nods. Words will not come. It is the first time in his life he has ever spoken to a neighbour. It is the first time he has ever been invited by anyone for a cuppa.

George goes to get some more hot water, while Julie

begins to chat with the two friends about nothing in particular, and gently but gently draws Colin into the conversation. He is stiff and uncomfortable, but no longer feels sick, and no longer wanting to make a bolt for it. He is on new ground, but though it felt strange, it also felt light and ever so slightly warm. He will be even warmer as the new climate grows on him.

The diva of St. Dunstan's

'Tucker in F. Agnes' said the diminutive conductor, peering over his half-moon glasses at the music stand in front of him. Half a dozen sopranos in the front row of the choir stalls began to shuffle their parts, while a chorus of 'Eh?' and 'What was that?' rumbled round the back rows of men. Victor the conductor raised his eyes to the organ loft and began silently waving his arms. After a few beats the first chords of the Agnus Dei emerged from the organ. The organist always knew what was coming next, as if by telepathy, and after a few familiar chords the more seasoned choristers already knew what to start singing even though they had not yet found the music.

Steven the tenor, who was new to all this, having been loaned from another choir, stared hard at his neighbour's music to see what it was, and opened his mouth to look as if he was singing, while he riffled through the pile of sheets that had been given him on the way in. He had just found the right page after about six bars, when Victor lowered his arms without a word and the choir stopped singing.

'Right, that'll do,' said Victor. 'Just wanted to remind

you of the opening. Don't forget to put the stress on the 'Ca' in Peccata.'

'But I hadn't even got that far!' whispered Steven to Arthur, his neighbour.

'I know, but he wants to get home for his tea. We've just had proper choir rehearsal, and this is extra for Geraldine's wedding on Saturday'

Geraldine's mum, Sonia, sat opposite, and kept looking at her watch, as Victor methodically pored over his service list, and turned to the next piece.

'Can you get a move on Victor. We've got another session with the dressmaker tonight.'

'Well, all right love, but we've only been started ten minutes' said Victor with a furrowed brow.

'Some of us have been here since half past six you know' she announced to the choir at large, as if it was anybody's fault but hers that they were here at all. She leaned forward and cast a baleful stare down the nave to where Geraldine, the bride to be, sat with a friend in a darkened and empty church. Geraldine raised her eyes heavenward and folded her arms heavily.

'OK then,' said Victor with a sigh. 'Let all mortal flesh keep silence.'

'And especially Geraldine's mum, eh' said Arthur, rather louder than was appropriate, and as a roll of unkind laughter overtook the tenors and basses, Sonia glared across at them with pursed lips.

Victor raised his arms and the organ began again, and once more Steven hurriedly shuffled his parts to find the matching one, and just made it to the first note. Again, no sooner had they started than Victor brought them to a halt.

'It says solo for the first eight bars,' said Sonia. The sopranos had already started to sing the first line in unison.

'Oh, you should have said, Victor' said Julie.

'I shouldn't have to say it if it's written down, should I?' Victor was gently polite even when he was being sarcastic.

'Well, who's singing it then? Julie went on. 'Shouldn't it be... you know... ?'

She meant the usual principal soprano, the diva of St Dunstan's, who now sat in the darkness halfway down the church. Her mum in the choir stalls nodded vigorously, looking expectantly at Victor.

'I know who it would be normally. But on this occasion,' Victor paused weightily. 'On this occasion I would like it to be in unison. OK?'

There was another heavy silence, as the sopranos looked at one another apprehensively.

'They already were in bloody unison,' muttered Arthur. Steve thought this an odd carry on, for the choir to ignore the instruction on the music, and the choirmaster to ignore the convention of the choir.

Victor raised his arms once more, the organist resumed the opening chords, and the sopranos began again the opening line.

'Let all mortal flesh keep silence...'

'Victor...'

It was Geraldine's mum, who had not been singing. She stood leaning on the music stand, with her copy closed. Victor dropped his arms, and the choir dribbled to a halt.

'Yes love?'

'Can I have a word?'

As this seemed to be not for public consumption, Victor was obliged to walk over to Sonia, wearing a pained look. He leaned towards her, and she whispered something in his ear.

'Oh, bloody hell, what now?' groaned Arthur, as the conversation opposite seemed somewhat strained, and Victor's normally calm demeanour began to be punctuated by fingers that repeatedly opened and closed, and a deal of shaking of the head. After a while he returned to the podium with his eyes to the ground, leaving a thunderstruck Sonia standing in confusion.

'Like I said,' Victor announced patiently. 'Unison'. And he raised his arms again. The choir picked up their parts and prepared to sing. The opening chords reappeared, and the women had just taken their first breath when Sonia's voice cut through the church.

'Geraldine!' she commanded.

Geraldine, who was in a quiet huddle with her friend, sat up and paid attention, as if by old habit. Victor lowered his arms. The organ stopped. Several of the men sat down pointedly and cast murderous looks around. Steven was even more confused.

'Geraldine!'

The girl walked quickly up to the choir stalls, and her mum met her at the foot of the steps. Victor stood between them. There was more tense whispering between the three of them. Though they could not hear what was being said, many of the choristers had a fair idea, and it seemed to Steven that Victor was being attacked from both sides, and that old battles were being re-fought. His demeanour became more and more dejected, and he was clearly not getting a word in.

Finally, he returned to his podium, collected his music and bag, said, 'Sorry ladies and gentlemen. Goodnight.' He walked off into the vestry, closely pursued by the two women.

There was an awkward silence, as the choir stood or sat in confusion, some delving into pockets for a Fisherman's Friend, one or two slipping out for a quick fag.

'What's happening?' Steven asked Arthur in alarm. He was getting used to pieces being rehearsed in short snippets, but when the choirmaster himself disappeared after only fifteen minutes, he thought these were strange customs indeed. The older man grunted in disgust.

'You wouldn't want to know, son, a nice lad like you.'

A voice from above broke through the awkward moment.

'Shall we carry on then?' the organist spoke brightly as if they had all just come back from a toilet break.

'Parry, page three, all right?' And he thundered into the intro to the second section. The choir quickly got the message and rustled their papers, coming in perfectly at the right moment.

Although the music was very loud, it was not quite loud enough to drown out the sounds of the furious row that was erupting in the vestry, which sounded to Steven like two cats squalling. One member got up while still singing, and crept out to close the vestry door.

After the rehearsal, as the choir gathered in the vestry, the usual conspiratorial huddles stood around, as several smokers lit up and coughed themselves back to normal health, while others continued singing while the mood lasted. Julie noticed Steven standing alone, and came over to him.

'How've you gone on then? Bit difficult I expect being thrown in at the deep end.'

'Well, I haven't done too badly,' he said, 'but I'm not sure what's going on,'

She took him to one side and brought her face close to his, speaking in a low voice.

'Geraldine and her mum go back a long way, you see. Mum used to be the principal soprano, and now its Geraldine. They think they run the choir, know what I mean? And now she's getting married, and they've chosen all the music themselves. But they can't think how the choir can manage without her in the lead.'

'Oh, I see.'

There was a polite coughing from nearby, and the hubbub died down. Robert the organist smiled weakly.

'If I can have your attention for a minute… I'm sorry about tonight, but I'm sure we can work something out. If, er, Victor doesn't come back, perhaps you, Andrew, wouldn't mind conducting the bits with the organ?'

Andrew, a senior chorister nodded.

'And I'll come down to conduct the unaccompanied numbers. What do you think?'

There was a murmur of assent, and the choir left their parts in the usual untidy piles, and drifted off, leaving the saintly Robert to clear up as usual.

*

Midday on Saturday, and Steven stood in the chancel among the choir, now angelically transformed in cassocks and white smocks, waiting for the bride. He was surprised to find that the choir was now almost doubled in size.

'Who are all these others?' he whispered to Arthur.

'They're t'regulars, and Geraldine's cronies' he replied sardonically.

'Don't they have to come to rehearsals?'

'Nah, lad, they know it all already'

'Is the choir master coming?'

'Couldn't tell you, son. She's ten minutes late already.'

'She… ?'

But Steven's worries were left unresolved, as the organ started up with the first chord of the introit, and a whisper went round – 'She's 'ere!' Arthur muttered, 'About bloody time.'

They began to sing, with Andrew the chorister beating time, as the clergy floated in amid candles and incense, the minister in gold trimmed robe, escorted by two acolytes holding up its corners. They were followed by the gorgeously attired Geraldine and her father, whom Steven hardly recognised from the plain young woman who sulked in the aisle on Friday night. The choir filed in pairs behind them, Steven hoping he would not trip on his borrowed cassock, which was three inches too long.

After a deal of time spent genuflecting and positioning round the altar, and the little man with the incense waving his smoking pot at all and sundry as if they needed fumigating, and everyone nodding at him in turn, the minister turned to the congregation and welcomed them

After the usual prefatory remarks he added, 'but this is an even more special occasion, because it is a very musical one. Not only have Geraldine and her mother chosen the music for the service, but they have one or two surprises in store'

Sonia could not prevent a smirk from appearing beneath her floral hat, Steven observed.

'Oh Lord!' muttered Arthur. 'What now?'

The ceremony took its usual course. The excessively well-scrubbed and over-dressed groom bore a look of delight and surprise at the moment his bride removed her veil, as if he had found a new woman. There were tears among many in the choir and congregation as the time hallowed words rolled around their memories, and deep sadness and longing among those for whom it had all turned sour.

Geraldine played her part to perfection. Even when the sopranos sang her solo part during the signing of the register, the smile never left her face. But, the formalities over, instead of remaining at the foot of the steps, Geraldine and her mother abandoned the rest of the party and made their way to the top of the choir, to sit in two carved wooden seats.

The minister rounded off the service with the appropriate prayers. The choir sang the Agnus Dei, and Steven noticed the two women singing along. Finally, the priest announced, 'The choir will sing the anthem, 'I was glad'

Andrew the deputy conductor got up to stand at the head of the choir, as the organ struck up the triumphant opening chords. But at the same time two things happened. Geraldine's mum left her seat and shuffled into the body of the choir, floral hat and all, into the position of the principal soprano, causing a flutter amongst the women, who all had to shove up one place.

And Geraldine marched up to the podium, plonked her bouquet into the arms of Andrew, and motioned him back to the choir stalls, grinning all over her face. As the organ introduction concluded, she hitched up her voluminous satin train, raised her arms and looked expectantly at the choir.

'I was glad…'

Twenty-five mouths opened wide, and twenty-five sets of eyes even wider. It was fortunate that most of them knew the words by heart, as none was able to find their place for several bars.

*

'Well, that's another one out of the way,' Julie said to Steven afterwards, as they disrobed in the vestry. 'What did you think of that?'

'I, um… it was…'

'Aye, I know what you mean,' she replied, 'just what I was thinking.'

'Where will they be going for their honeymoon,' he asked, wanting to change the subject.

'Paris, I think they said. But only for a week though.'

'Oh that sounds romantic. Pity it's not longer, though.'

'Aah. She'll not want to stay any longer, our Geraldine.'

'Why not?'

'Well, she'll want to be back for next Sunday's service, won't she. Can't let a little thing like getting married interrupt her routine.'

Danny's dish

'Mmmm, I *love* chocolate, Mr Hart!'

'I know. You keep telling me.'

Mr Hart grinned at the double chin and roly-poly frame of Danny.

'Just make sure you keep those fingers out of your mouth.'

'Yeah. Because... because... Mrs Jackson told us... all our germs might get in someone's tummy.'

Ten fifteen-year-old cooks clattered about, in animated conversation, while two teachers flitted nervously between them, like jugglers spinning plates on sticks, trying to keep each one in turn from crashing to the floor. Tanya's group were fiddling with the food processor and two pints of double cream. Four lanky lads scraped manfully at a mountain of potatoes, their brows furrowed in concentration. Danny was hopping from foot to foot and drooling with lust as he and Sophie broke several lumps of chocolate into a bowl.

The whole day was devoted to this task, all normal teaching abandoned. With military efficiency, Mrs Jackson had taken them through the whole process in the last three weeks of preparing for the annual Christmas feast for the staff of the special school and invited guests. This was the day. The day for last minute things.

'I can't wait to eat this!' said Danny for the fifth time. 'Sophie...'

Sophie was dolloping butter into the weighing tray, with her tongue between her lips, totally absorbed in the feel and sound of it.

'Sophie...'

'What?'

'I can't wait to eat this.'

'Well, you'll have to Danny,' Mr Hart said. 'Even when the puddings are served, you'll have to wait till all the guests have got theirs. In fact, they might like it so much there might not be any left for you.'

Danny's face fell, and then he saw the twinkle in Mr Hart's eye.

'There will!' he protested.

'Oh, I don't know. We'll have to wait and see. That's what waiters do, Danny. Wait.'

'How long will we have to wait?'

'Oh, ages I should think.' Mr Hart laid it on thick. 'I mean I shall certainly want two helpings, and Mrs Jackson will. And I have known Mr Smith have three when he really likes something.'

'He won't will he?' Danny's chubby face wrinkled with concern.

Sophie was still piling up the butter, and frowning at the dial.

'Is it this line or that one?' she asked, not knowing which was pounds and which was grams. She had already reached two pounds, and she was aiming for 100 grams.

'I think you've overdone it a bit, Sophie.'

Mr Hart scooped up half the butter and put it in another dish before she had time to notice how big her mistake was.

Piling the chocolate, butter and syrup into one bowl they set off towards the microwave. Returning a few minutes later with a bowl of warm bubbly goo, Danny watched gleefully as Sophie tipped it into the flour and fruit.

'Can I mix it Mr Hart, please?' he begged.

'Why can't you be so keen when we do normal work, Danny?' Mr Hart thought of the usual boy slumped over the page, yawning and scratching and puzzling, and saying, 'What time is it?'

Danny grinned. 'I *love* chocolate!'

'Yes but, said Mr Hart. 'but,you might not like the pudding when its finished.'

*

Mr Hart didn't see them for the rest of the day, but the group toiled on, working through breaks, not wanting to go out at lunch time, falling out, laughing and joking. Only two dishes were broken, and not many foods had to be scraped off the floor. Much washing up was endured with a good grace. Normal rules were suspended. All were held in thrall at the prospect of a once in a lifetime experience of a full-blown sit down meal in five courses, with a properly laid table, with cutlery (cutlery, miss, what's that?), and named labels, wine glasses and napkins.

Mr Hart turned up that evening in a suit and tie, and there was mutual astonishment when Sophie met him at the door looking quite extraordinary, and his mouth dropped when she said, 'Can I take your coat, sir?'

She was wearing a dress. He noticed her legs for the first time. In tights. Sophie awkwardly relieved him of his coat, and showed him to an armchair by a low table bearing flowers. Here sat several other teachers all looking equally bemused.

Hartley School was a grand Victorian edifice, with a spacious entrance hall. The main floor of the hall was transformed by the presence of a long linen clad dining table, neatly set with place mats, festive decorations and tall glasses.

A huddle of students waited gawkily near the door, like former ugly ducklings who had just looked into a mirror and found they had turned into swans. Mr Smith waited with them, and nudged one into action each time another guest walked in. There was much giggling and pointing at the teachers who had risen to the challenge and dressed to kill. While they in turn raised discreet eyebrows and smiled ironically as they tried to take in the new comely young adults who were the bane of their lives by day.

After a while someone banged on a tray upstairs. The guests looked up, as a posse of pupils clumped down the stairs. Among them was Danny, who gave a radiant smile as he saw Mr Hart, and said, 'You gotta come with me sir.'

He looked years older in a jacket, shirt and tie. He grabbed his arm, and pulled him by the sleeve till he reached a place at the table.

'You sit there,' he ordered. 'See, it says Mr Hart.' He held the label under Mr Hart's nose. Then as his guest made to sit down, he said, 'Just a minute!' and grabbed the chair from him, pulled it back and waited for him to stand in front of it.

'Thank you, Danny'

'Do you know what we got to eat?'

Danny forgot that just a few hours ago and every day for the last three weeks his guest had been helping him to prepare the meal.

'No Danny, tell me.'

'Look,' he said, 'this is the menu.'

He proudly showed him the list of courses on offer, which he himself had helped to print on the computer. Mr Hart expressed his admiration.

'What do you want first?'

'What do you recommend?'

'Eh?'

'What do *you* think's the best?'

'I made this one.'

Danny proudly pointed to the prawn and ginger salad.

'I'll try that then, said Mr Hart graciously. Danny's chest swelled in his brother's jacket as he almost ran to fetch his first order.

Since it was no longer used as a house, there was no dining room, and so the kitchen where cookery was taught was actually upstairs. This meant that all the food had to be brought downstairs one item at a time. But since in this case there were a dozen servants, labour was cheap, and the whole evening was orchestrated by the thunderous clattering of platform soles which were the height of teenage fashion in that year, on the fifty odd un-carpeted wooden steps.

Two girls in particular, Julie and Roxanne, who could never be separated, were treated as a serving twin, and they shared the portage of all the major dishes, stomping in unison, so that the arrival of the turkey was heralded by marching hammer blows. The staff cottoned on very quickly, and before they reached the foot of the stairs, the whole party was clapping in time to the girls' feet, and its arrival was greeted with a mighty cheer.

In the meantime, polite conversation amongst the guests was conducted at shouting pitch, as the cavernous hall echoed to the percussive efforts of the servants. It only quietened between courses, when the servants became guests, and had their own portions of their own preparations.

One lad, Faisal, who had no speech, was encouraged to tap on the shoulders of the diners to offer them portions of bread, which was one way of making him feel involved. When he himself sat down, the guest teacher beside him helped him to cut up his food and eat it without mess, as if it were his own toddler at home. No-one batted an eyelid, and the conversation flowed uninterrupted.

'Sir...'

'Yes, Danny?'

'Guess what I'm having for pudding?'

'Fruit salad?'

'Nooo!' Danny looked scandalized.

'Cheese and biscuits.'

'Nooo! That's not pudding!'

'Well, I can't guess.'

'Chocolate pudding!' Danny's eyes shone.

'What – that one we made together? Never!'

'I am! I can't wait. I love chocolate!'

'Well let's hope there's some left when it's your turn Danny.'

There was a flurry of activity near the door, where all the main courses had been arranged on small tables, and the gang of servants fanned out round the table to invite guests to help themselves at the carvery. As the woodwork teacher hacked away at the enormous turkey, Mr Hart surveyed the rest of the fare on offer. There was a huge variety of cultural tastes to cater for. Meat, non-meat, Asian, West Indian, English, diabetic, allergic. All had been accounted for. But in the end everyone had something they enjoyed. Tradition was thrown to the wind. Staff and students piled their plates high with just about everything they could get their hands on.

Mr Hart felt the stress of the last few weeks begin to fall away as he surveyed the scene. Opposite was Danny, cheeks puffed with too much roast potato, his tie all askew, struggling to loosen his belt. Down there Faisal stared vacantly as his minder guided another fork of meat past his dribbling lips. Julie and Roxanne talked and talked and ate simultaneously, as they did in most lessons. Though born in separate wombs, they were predestined to be choreographed as a comic duo, shuffling off any interference by teachers or future husbands.

There were big sister's lace blouses too long in the sleeve that did not conceal small adolescent bosoms. There were ballooning bosoms and buttocks that nothing could conceal. There were faces grossly made up, and faces made entirely of pimples. There were little boys in big men's jackets, and little skirts on big girl's thighs.

Danny was having trouble disposing of all he had piled on his plate, and when he went to clear the table for the arrival of the puddings, another student came in his absence and took his plate away. Just as well, thought Mr Hart. He looks fit to burst. This time instead of self-service they were plied once again by the young waiters, who, having crashed up the stairs rattling empty plates, now crashed down again carrying full pudding dishes. And grinning from ear to ear, a vast rotund chocolate pudding named Danny.

He watched anxiously as orders were taken, and slice after slice was removed, served up and consumed. There were indeed second helpings, and he could barely refrain from removing the pudding in case it should disappear before reaching his own plate.

But finally, as the first flush of pudding lust subsided, the students got their chance, and Danny actually ran down to the end of the table to secure his slice. He returned to his seat in great excitement.

'Look what I got sir!'

'The big moment, eh?'

Danny's desire had become common knowledge among

staff and students over the last few days, as he had gone round telling everyone who would listen. Now those who sat nearest downed spoons and watched. One even had a phone ready to take a picture.

'Mmmmmm!'

Danny's hand trembled as he carved into the solid and shiny sides of his large slice. The combination of chocolate treacle and fruit made it look more like a piece of black pudding. He stuffed the first spoonful in his mouth and chewed.

Then he stopped chewing. The camera flashed and caught him with his cheek bulged and a furrowed brow. The onlookers held their breath and waited.

'Nnnnn.' A strangled grunt.

'What's up Danny?'

'Its 'orrible!' said Danny.

'Mm mm mm'

He searched the table for a napkin. Someone saw what was coming and passed him one. He grabbed it like a drowning man. His mouth opened, and he filled the napkin with as much grace as he could muster.

His friends were less discreet.

'Uuuugh! Danny!'

'Its 'orrible!' said Danny again

'Oh Danny, what a shame, after all that.' Mr Hart tried to keep a straight face, and several other staff turned away and carried on as if nothing had happened.

'What shall I do with this, sir?'

Danny indicated the remaining pudding on his plate.

'Oh, I should wrap it in a clean napkin and take it home

for your mum. She'll want to see what you worked so hard on, won't she.'

'Will it make her sick?'

'Shouldn't think so, Danny,' said Mr Hart, who himself had avoided the pudding. 'Some things you don't like when you're young, but you change your mind about when them when you get older.'

And while Sophie concentrated furiously on not spilling the cup of tea she was bringing him afterwards, he noticed the forlorn face of Danny rising up the stairs as he carried a pile of dirty dishes.

Dear, delightful, open hearted, disappointed Danny, pudding maker.

Carnival

As the day of the carnival approached, there was a hum of purposeful activity among the residents of the little market town of Rumblington. At the Dripping Tap, the oldest regulars gathered around the log fire which burned summer and winter, supping their pints of Old Particular, and swapping tales of carnivals of yore. Tappists to a man, they had all played their part in the fund raising, and manning of floats, and a few had played in the Tappist band, which traditionally led the procession from the town centre into the park. Some still carried their polished black and brass ferruled canes, symbol of Tappist pride, and principal feature of the marching band's livery.

This year the talk was intermittent, and there was an absence of laughter. In the spaces between utterances, burned a silence of frustration. The Tappists were not pleased. The comfortable cushion of old custom had been whipped from under them. The object of their anger was the Bombles.

'I can't see the point of it.' said Fred, tapping his cane on the hearth on the word 'point'. A murmur of sympathy erupted from his companions. 'Tha's the way we always done it, ever since I was a boy. Why we gotta change it round now, I ask you?'

'That ain't just since we was boys, Fred,' added Bert,' That goes back five hundred and twenty three year,' referring to the Battle of Rumblington in 1377.

'Ah, so it do, tha's right,' rumbled round the group. A long silence followed, interrupted only by a further tap from Fred's cane, in the place of words that could not be found.

Meanwhile on the other side of the town square this lunchtime, the residents of the Bomble Bee were in quite a different mood. Here was a younger crowd, which included some women, and a few smart suits. Their roots in the community went almost as deep, but until now, to be a Bomble was to be an incomer.

This year, all that was about to change, thanks to the narrow victory of the Bombles in the town council elections, and the casting vote of the chairman of the Ways and Means committee, a local businessman, who ran a building company. They had decided that the Bomble Band, who had formerly always brought up the rear of the procession, this year would be in the lead, and the Tappists in the rear. This would not only break a five-hundred-year-old tradition, but would also give the financial advantage to the Bombles, since most people had run out of money to throw into the collecting buckets by the time the end of the procession came by.

And what was worse, they had taken note of the complaints of the residents of Duke Street, who felt intimidated by the Tappist habit of double tapping their canes on the pavement on the Bomble side of the street as they passed, and waving them in the air between taps. The procession was to be re-routed, it was rumoured!

'What do you reckon then?' asked Justin of the handful of well-heeled lager drinkers around the pool table. 'Will they swallow it?'

'Doubt it,' said Kevin, 'not without a few sweeteners.' And he slammed the blue into a corner pocket.

'Can we afford it?'

'Can we afford not to? How long do we have to go on being second class citizens, because of some damned victory with sticks and staves in a medieval scrap.'

The headlines in the *Rumblington Echo* told the tale in shorthand in the days leading up the carnival.

June 2	CARNIVAL COMMITTEE IN UPROAR. POLICE CALLED IN.
June 3	COMMITTEE CHAIRMAN RESIGNS IN NO CONFIDENCE MOTION
June 4	NO CARNIVAL THIS YEAR? THREAT. DUKE ST RESIDENTS IN PROTEST OUTSIDE TOWN HALL
June 5	TAPPISTS BOYCOTT COUNCIL MEETING. 'NO COMPROMISE' – LODGE LEADER

In this edition a photograph of the Tappist Band marching around the Town Hall.

| June 6 | BOMBLES AND TAPPISTS IN SECRET TALKS |

	'WE WILL NOT BE INTIMIDATED' – DUKE ST RESIDENTS
June 7	BOMBLES AND TAPPISTS – TALKS CONTINUE
	WINDOWS SMASHED ON BOMBLE ESTATE.
June 8	IT'S A DEAL! CARNIVAL GOES AHEAD

The editor had taken the unusual step of not publishing the details of the final deal, perhaps in the interest of achieving a good sale for his paper on the day after the carnival.

The day of the carnival began in typical style, with lowering clouds and fitful wind, causing many a rueful glance at the sky from the occupants of the many floats, who were busy tightening up guy ropes and pennants and banners, in case of storm damage. Lining the streets of Rumblington were more than the usual crowd of onlookers, who shivered in the mid-day chill. They stretched from the Town Hall Square to the park, via Duke Street. Many were puzzled at 11am by the absence of floats and bands in the usual starting place. At the Park end of the route, where the procession usually wound up, there was more puzzlement, since the Park was full of floats and bands, and some wondered if the procession had already taken place.

The confusion was made worse when two streams of uniformed musicians marched silently out of the Park Gates and lined up on either side of the road. The white and black sashed Tappists with their canes on the left, the orange and blue striped Bombles with their ostrich feathered three cornered hats on the right. Both bands, at a short whistle from the leader of a posse of white frocked schoolgirls, held up their instruments ready to play. At a second whistle, drummers on both sides of the road struck up a roll, and at a third whistle, a marching rhythm. Both set off together to the sound of the drums.

After about a hundred steps the band of the Tappists began the first phrase of 'The White and the Black'. After thirty-two bars they stopped. At which the band of the Bombles began with 'The Blue and the Orange'. Following on were an assortment of uniformed marchers, some of whom carried collecting buckets, which they held up to the crowds. They were followed out of the park by the whole procession of floats, who came in alternate order of allegiance.

At Duke Street the residents were lined up on their respective sides of the street in silence. Their flags and banners flapped in the wind in equal turbulence. As the bands approached, they stopped playing any music two streets away, but the drummers both continued to provide the beat. The cane bearers of the Tappists held their canes across their chests. The ostrich feathers were also held against the chests of the Bombles, who walked on the Tappist side of the street, the Tappists on the Bomble side.

As they passed out of the street, the drumming continued on both sides until a further street was covered, and then the band which was not the last one to play, struck up again with another phrase from their chosen anthem. They continued with alternate music up to the Town Hall end of the route. Here there was a change of tactic. Both bands now began to play popular tunes of the day simultaneously, but they now split, and marched round the Town Hall in opposite directions. There was a minute of interesting harmonic confusion, as they passed on the other side.

Coming together again, after three more turns round the building, they resumed their marching, and carefully avoiding the last of the floats who had just arrived, made their way back again to the park. This time, each band was on the opposite side of the road to which they had come. In this way, neither had to bring up the rear, and the cash collectors had equal access to all members of the community. Both sides of Duke Street were served by both factions, the musicians gladly ceased competing with each other, and the silent procession began again on the way back, accompanied only by the drummers.

However, neither side was pleased with the compromise, because on the return journey, most people had not stayed to watch them a second time, and had gone off with their money to the various attractions at the park, where the stallholders celebrated a record turn-out.

BATTLE OF RUMBLINGTON – PEACE BREAKS OUT, said the *Echo* next day.

The old men at the Dripping Tap still sat around the fire. There was little to argue about. The frustration seemed muted, and for the first time in years Fred had left his cane at home, a fact which went unremarked by his mates, some of whom had done the same.

'What d'ya reckon then?' The landlord asked of Fred.

'Phwaaaw!' said Fred, and spat into the log fire.

At the Bomble Bee there was also little trade, following an all-night barbecue and disco, which left both staff and customers exhausted.

'What d'ya reckon then?' asked Kevin of Justin.

'Well takings were up on last year,' he said with a smile.

'And din't you just love that bit when the bands played two different songs at the same time?'

There was a ripple of laughter round the bar, amongst the few younger Bombles who had come to gloat.

At the next meeting at the Town Hall, the Chairman of the Ways and Means Committee was given a vote of thanks. He smiled graciously, as he thought of the new extension to his warehouse, which would soon be erected after all, despite adverse planning regulations.

Blackbird diplomacy

Marisa and her husband enter the old church hall in some trepidation. The spring sunshine gives life to the daffodils sprinkled among the old grave stones that line the long path to the Victorian church. A blackbird sings melodiously, from his perch high up in an ancient tree. But when they enter the room there is cool and a faint smell of damp. The lights serve only to lift the darkness a little in a room which even on a bright day like this, clings to its natural gloom.

Marisa feels unsure of herself. They have been asked here by the mediators to talk to their neighbours about the noise created by her children. She knows she is not fully in control of her four and two year old, who are quarrelsome, but to her, just like normal children. She is scared that the neighbours are using the situation to express something more than just annoyance over children. They are a generation older than her. They are English, who have lived here a long time. She is a young Polish woman, who has only been here a few months.

Radig stays close to his pretty wife as they approach the

table, around which are their neighbours and the two mediators, who already seem to be in a jovial conversation about something. He is as nervous as she is, with the additional knowledge that his English is only half as good as hers. His experience of the children is less troublesome, as he only sees them at the beginning and end of each day, when he is not working. He is reluctant to be here, in a strange and archaic English religious building, such as he has never entered in his life. He hardly has any knowledge of the neighbours except that they are upsetting his wife when he is not there. But he feels the need to defend the woman he loves. The two mediators rise and shake hands with both of them, and offer them tea and biscuits. The two neighbours smile warmly. Radig relaxes just a little.

Jane sits beside her husband. She has had ten minutes with the mediators, who have been subtly warming them up with trivial chatter about nuisance phone calls and difficult dogs. In their original talk with the mediators in her home, they had laid it on thick about screaming children, thin walls and fractious relationships between their dog and next door's. She is annoyed because she has been there, done it all before, and had no trouble with *her* children, who are now at college. She can't see why this young girl can't control her own kids like she used to do. She likes to read, sit in the garden, and listen to the birds. She also feels protective of her husband, who works long hours, and needs his rest when he comes home. Nevertheless she manages a warm greeting when the two young people arrive.

Darren sees himself as a solid guy, salt of the earth, a

long-term resident, whose life ran on smooth rails until this young Polish couple come along, and upset his routine. His experience of fatherhood had been one of discipline and order, he thinks. He had been in control. When a family arrives who not only clearly have no control over their children or their dog, and what's more, come from a culture he does not understand, he is at a loss as to how to deal with it. He and his wife sit many an evening and early morning fuming over the noise from next door, and the fact that their houses have such thin walls that they can hear every word of a phone conversation from their neighbours.

Having greeted the two young people George begins to chat briefly about the problems they have had with recorded messages when trying to contact them. He notes that the couple had installed a system which prevents them from receiving calls from unknown persons. This had frustrated him, and until they walked in the door, he did not know whether they would turn up. Why would they need to do this? He keeps it in the back of his mind in case it has some bearing on the case.

His colleague Harriet, is as calm as a millpond, and has the ability to talk to him and to everyone else in such a tone that they all feel good in her company. She has years of dealing with difficult children and knows the stresses that their young parents experience. But she is not here to counsel anyone or offer advice, and enjoys the neutrality of the mediator position, in which she has the knowledge, but is not expected to reveal it.

George asks Darren and Jane to speak first. Each pair is

asked not to interrupt while they state their case. He can see that Jane has a file in front of her, which looks like a long list of incidents.

Surprisingly Darren sets off with a completely new topic.

'Did you know that when you sit in your garden smoking, Marisa, the smoke comes straight in my kitchen window while I'm cooking?'

This was news to Marisa and the two mediators, and he had not mentioned it to them before. A secret weapon he had kept hidden with which to disarm them right at the start.

He takes the paper they had laid out and proceeds to draw a map of their houses and gardens. His kitchen is nearest to the fence between the two houses. Marisa's smoking place is right next to it.

Marisa is taken off guard.

'I didn't know that. You never said before. I am sorry. What can I do? I did have a year off smoking when I was pregnant, but now I feel so stressed a lot of the time.' She looks at her husband fearfully. He does not respond.

George says something about the prevailing wind in his street, which always tells him when his neighbour is out smoking. He asks Marisa what she thinks she could do.

'I will move my seat to the other side of the garden,' she offers. Darren thanks her. One little victory to him. Harriet scribbles this down in her checklist of agreements.

Darren presses on. 'It's not the dogs any more, love. That seems to be under control now,' he says, using that key word to imply judgment. 'They used to be snarling at each other all the time when they were in the garden. And yours doesn't whine any more like it used to do in the house.' He is laying it on a bit thick.

'No, he doesn't,' says Marisa, 'but I don't know what changed'

This is two bullet points to Darren, and he notes the effect on her nerves.

George asks, 'Shall we take that off the list then?' He is glad too, as the control of dogs, or lack of it, is a perennial subject of mediation. Harriet crosses it out from her list. Smiles all round.

'But when I come home, all I want to do is sit quietly for half an hour, and relax. But that's when the screaming and crying seems to get worse,' Darren continues. 'And the stamping and running about. Do you know the floor shakes and some ornaments wobble?' He demonstrates with his hands.

Jane chips in before Marisa has a chance to respond.

'I like to sit in the garden and read, but the other day I was doing that and you put your radio in the window so we could all hear the music in the garden. Were you doing that on purpose, Marisa?'

Marisa is feeling more and more disarmed and depressed.

'No, Jane, I didn't know you were there, or I would not have done it. I wouldn't do that on purpose. I am sorry.'

'Can we leave that aside for a moment?' Harriet intervenes. She feels bad that they have allowed this sequence of attacks at this stage in the process.

'I would like to concentrate on the situation with the

children. Marisa, tell us how it is with the children.'

She chooses neutral phrases so as to avoid any feeling of judgment on Marisa. Marisa glances at her husband, who has said very little so far. She wishes he would support her.

'Hannah is four and Egon is two. When they are together, he will take a toy that she is playing with, and he wants to do what she is doing. Then she screams, and I say – Don't scream, stop screaming – and she gets worse. She stamps and throws things about, and even if I hold her, she will not stop. I don't know what to do.'

'Is it always you and Hannah,' George asks, 'when she is like this? What happens when Radig is there?'

'She is better for me,' says Radig at last. 'But I only see them at end of day. Marisa has to have them all time.'

'Yes, we noticed,' Darren chips in, wanting to press home his advantage. 'When you come home things get a lot quieter.'

Marisa casts her eyes down. She feels she is being accused of being a bad mother.

Radig goes on, 'When Marisa mother come round, Hannah is well behaved. But she only come about once a month.'

Harriet pursues this.

'Do you know why that is so, Marisa? Have you talked to your mother about it?'

'She, my mother and I, we don't get on very well. And she is working also…' There are tears in her eyes.

George asks if she would like a break. Marisa leaves the room quickly, closely followed by Radig. The rest all grab a bottle of water or a biscuit and George puts the kettle on.

The incident seems to have a softening effect on Jane, who gets up to put her arms around Marisa when she returns.

'It's all right, love, we understand.'

Harriet continues. 'Marisa, Does Hannah go to nursery?'

'She goes for three hours every morning.'

'Is she well behaved there?'

'She is no trouble at nursery.'

'Have you talked to any of the other mothers about her behaviour?'

'No,' says Marisa, 'I don't know any of them. They don't speak to me.'

Another stick to beat me with, she thinks.

'Now why would that be?' thinks George to himself.

'I think if you asked the staff, they might be able to tell you about any mother and toddler groups. Would you think it would be useful to share your experience with some other mums?'

'That's what I used to do when mine were little,' Jane chips in. 'How about if I were to come down there with you one day? We could ask together, couldn't we.' She sees a girl on the ropes, and feels the need to rescue her.

'Yeah!' thinks George. 'Come on Marisa!'

Through the window in the roof of the dingy church hall comes the sound of the blackbird singing the spring.

Radig added, 'I think that sound good Marisa.'

Marisa smiles, and her whole body seems to loosen up, as she meets the gaze of Jane, who seems to have come onto her side.

'Yes, I would like that. Thank you.' Tears spring up again, but Jane reaches across and lays her hand on Marisa's. Harriet makes a mental note of this.

'Are you both renting your house from the council?' George enquires. They are both tenants.

'Shall we talk about the building? Sounds like your insulation is not so good.'

Radig adds 'I look at that. It was going to be thirty thousand pounds to insulate the walls'

'But' George continues, 'Jane has been asked to keep a list of all the times that she has been disturbed by the noise. Has that been helpful, Jane?' He wishes he could have phrased it better.

Jane smiles, and with her hand on the notebook she has brought, says, 'No, you're right love. It's not made any difference.' She puts it back in her bag.

'What do you think would help then?'

'I tell you what's been helpful, love, it's been us sitting here listening to Marisa and Radig. I've fair felt for her, you know. We've never sat down and really talked about things. We've just sat in our houses and moaned about each other.'

'This is true,' Marisa adds, 'I have been so afraid about upsetting them, and not being able to control my children. It's made me more miserable. But now I feel we could become friends.'

This was the key moment that George and Harriet looked for in every mediation, when the feuding parties have moved each other so much that they really start to listen to each other.

'So,' says George. 'Is there one practical step you can

take to deal with the soundproofing?'

Darren, having rye-ly observed his wife's sudden burst of empathy, is by now in a different place from where he came in, and he pipes up.

'Tell you what love. How about you both go down to't council and ask to talk to someone about insulation?'

George remembers something useful.

'Sometimes, you know, we do mediations about buildings. They have a man called the Disrepair Officer.' This brings smiles of disbelief all round.

The blackbird continues to illuminate the room with its beautiful territorial boundary marking, while inside six bodies notably more relaxed than two hours ago, sit and chat about less serious things. Harriet and George draw up what they think has been agreed. After signing, the four neighbours slowly stroll into the sunshine, chatting amiably. The two mediators smile at each other, do the washing up, write their notes, and then sit outside in the sunshine, waiting for the return of the caretaker, while the blackbird sings on, regardless.

A tale of two dogs

'It's the dog,' Jo says, red in the face. 'I hear him shouting at it, and swearing. A dog shouldn't be treated like that. And I heard him throw the dog across the room!'

Two tears trickle down her cheeks.

'How do you know it was the dog he threw?' asks George calmly.

'Because I heard it squeal when it hit the floor,' she says, 'and it upset me so much.' By now she is gulping and sobbing with the emotion of it.

'She's right you know,' says her cousin Peter, 'I heard it too. It makes my dog bark as well. You know how dogs react to one another.'

'You've got a dog too?' says George.

'Aye, and I wouldn't treat mine as bad as that, or I wouldn't be fit to have a dog.'

Jo recovers herself a little.

'There was one day he brought it down to the lawn outside my flat to do its business, and he leaned against my window and shouted at the dog. I opened the window and asked him if he'd mind standing somewhere else, so he went and stood by the tree. He told me to fuck off.'

'Was that the first time you'd spoken to him?' Sarah, George's fellow mediator, chips in.

'Well because I can't get out much, we hardly ever see each other.'

Jo puts her hand on her walking frame. 'I can't walk much you see, because of me back problem.'

Peter adds a bit more. 'The four flats are kind of set up so our doors are not too close. Its only if he comes down the stairs when we're goin' out that we'd ever bump into each other.'

'And you've been there about nine months?' Sarah asks,' and was that the first time you'd actually seen him face to face Jo?'

'I don't want to see him. He's a nasty man, and I'm scared of him.' Tears start to roll again.

'What about the lady? You've not met her either?'

'Jo is virtually house bound,' says Peter. 'She can't go out much, unless someone takes her, and that's usually me or her mum.'

'But I hear 'em,' says Jo. 'I can hear almost everything they say, because the flats are not sound proof. And it's when he's there they shout. And the dog gets upset. And when they go out they leave it in a sort of a cage, and it whines all the time. Sometimes into the early hours, and it keeps me awake, you know. I can't stand it!'

By now Jo is in a state of misery, wiping her tears with a tissue and blowing her nose. Peter just stares at her helplessly. It is hard to tell what their relationship might be, but it doesn't look very warm.

'Shall we have a little break? Would you like a drink?' says George. But the two of them decline.

'No, I just want to get this over with,' says Jo through her tears.

'It's the banging too,' Peter goes on. 'They keep banging doors all the time, and he keeps stamping about.'

'When you say all the time,' says George, 'how often are we talking about?'

Banging doors all the time, is a refrain he hears so often in mediation, he wonders if there is a certain type of restless human being who gets a kick out of it, or who is incapable of closing a door quietly.

'Well, we know when they're in the kitchen,' Jo continues, ''cos of the cupboard doors banging, and moving from one room to another, and when they come in and go out, they bang the doors.'

'But how often are they in the kitchen would you say?' Sarah ventures, thinking how little she herself might inhabit that corner of the house.

'Oh, half a dozen times a day,' says Peter. 'They can't seem to do anything quietly.'

'Has either of you spoken to them about it?'

'I told Council about it,' says Jo sheepishly.

'And what happened then?' asks Sarah.

'They came and spoke to them and us.'

'Did anything change?'

'For about one day they were quiet. And then it started up again.' Peter's pale face shows no sign of any emotion.

'I called the police.' Jo says bitterly.

'What, about the banging?' George asks.

'No, about the dog,' she continues. 'I couldn't stand it any more, so I called police.'

'And what did they do?'

'They asked us to keep a list of all the times when we heard them mistreating the dog.' Jo reaches into her handbag and offers a piece of paper to George.

'So did they make a difference?' George asks, ignoring the paper, and knowing the answer already.

'Not a bit. That poor dog…' Jo's tears start to flow again.

*

George and Sarah are taking the unusual step of seeing both parties and the final meeting all on one afternoon in the one building. They are careful to keep the parties in different rooms. Now they have in front of them the other couple, Harry and Teresa, and another woman, who turns out to be Harry's mother.

'I've come to support my son,' she says firmly. 'He's a carer for another lady, but he needs a lot of care himself.'

Harry is quite small, and looks about twenty, although he must be at least thirty-five. He is rather dwarfed by Teresa his partner, who looks uncomfortable in her bulky frame.

George and Sarah do their usual mental snapshot of the couple and the situation with the mother, and a red flag flutters in the picture. They thank them all for coming, but say they were expecting just the two couples.

'I know love,' says Tracey the mother, 'but I've heard what's goin' on myself, so I thought it might be helpful to be here.'

George sort of half turns his body towards Harry, to indicate to mum that it is him that he wants to speak to now.

'You are in the flat upstairs I believe. How long have you been there?'

'About a year,' Teresa speaks for him. 'And it were all right when we first come. But then *she* started causin' trouble.'

'By *she* you mean… ?' George enquires.

''er downstairs of course. Don't know 'er name.'

'They are Jo and Peter,' Sarah adds. 'Have you not met them yet?'

'They don't ever go out, do they. Never said 'ello or owt like that. But Harry had a bit of a do wi' 'er like, when 'e took dog down one day, din't yer love?'

'Aye, I were talkin' to't dog on't grass, and she opened winder and shouted at me to move away. She said I were treatin' 't dog badly. I told 'er to mind 'er own business like.'

'Was that the first time you spoke to her Harry?' Sarah asks.

'Ay, an' it might well be 't last too.' Harry is working up a bit of steam now, and catches the eye of his mother, who nods and grins.

'How did that make you feel, Harry?'

Harry stops to think for some time. He is not used to being asked about his feelings. He just feels them, and reacts accordingly. Sarah waits patiently.

'You were fair upset, were'nt yer love,' Mother tips in.

'Harry?'

'Aye, I were fair upset like,' Harry has grabbed some words.

'So how did that make you feel about Jo then?'

'Well, she were a right nasty bugger. No need to talk to someone like that who you don't even know.'

Teresa chips in. 'After that there were a letter from 't council about noise. I said to 'im (nodding at Harry), noise, what noise? Din't I. An' they come round to talk to us. It were bangin', and shoutin' at dog, they said. Bangin', I said, what bangin'? An' she said doors and stampin about like. We don't stamp about do we 'arry, and we certainly don't shout at dog, why would we do that?'

'Do you shout at the dog, Harry?' George asks.

'Well, y'ave to be a bit firm wi'em don't yer,' Harry replies, 'A Staffy needs a bit o' firm 'andlin like.'

Mum pops up again. 'Tell 'em about their dog 'arry, what you told me.' She speaks as if Teresa were not there.

'They 'ave a dog as well, don't know what sort. But it barks like most dogs do. If my dog barks, then 'ers'll bark as well, like dogs do. '

'But we don't complain about that, do we,' Teresa snorts. 'We all know what dogs are like. You'd think she ought to know that, don't yer think?'

'Where do you keep the dog, Harry?' George is aware of Jo's concern about the dog late at night.

'It 'as run o't flat when we're in. But when we go out 'e 'as like a sort of cage in't kitchen where 'e sleeps. 'E's no trouble.'

'What did the Council person say about the dog noises Teresa?' Sarah tries to move the focus to the female side.

'She said summat about barkin' and whinin' when we're out. But 'e din't used to do that where we lived before.'

'You mean nobody complained about it?'

'Yeah. But we 'ad a bit o' garden there like.'

'And the dog stayed outside at night?'

'Yeah. We 'ad a kennel for 'im.'

'And do you take him out for walks?'

'Aye,' says Harry,' he goes wi' me when I go out on my carin' job.'

Tracey chips in. 'Tell 'em about RSPCA, lad.'

Teresa takes the initiative to avoid this becoming mother in law's show.

'We 'ad RSPCA round and they said they couldn't find any marks on the dog, and no sign of distress, and we was doin' all right wi' 'im, dint they 'arry.'

'And what about police?' Tracey again. George feels she is whipping up a storm here in defence of her son.

'Were the police involved Harry? What was that about?'

'They said it were a complaint about cruelty to animals,' Harry begins, but is interrupted by Teresa, 'And that was why we 'ad RSPCA round.'

'And what happened then?'

'Nothin'. I don't know if they went to see 'er downstairs, but nothin' appened.'

Teresa folds her arms and sighs.

'It's this callin' out police and council what bothers them,' says Tracey, 'that's what so annoyin'. And they're not doin' owt wrong.'

*

'What do you reckon then?' George looks at Sarah after they have shepherded the couple to their own room.

'We can't have Mum in it can we. She'd wreck it.'

'You're right. Would you like to ask her, or shall I?'

'I'll do it,' she says. 'But what do you think about Jo? Should we keep letting her cry like that?'

'If we don't, we could be all day,' says George.' I think we just have to accept that's how she's gonna be. I'll talk to her.'

So, while Sarah goes to sweet talk the mother, George does the same for Jo. Surprisingly Jo tells him she wants to get it over with, because she can't stand things as they are.

*

When they all get together, Sarah has arranged for a jug of water and six glasses, which she begins to share out while George goes through the routine preliminaries of a joint meeting. They sit in a triangle, with George and Sarah facing two couples who are at ninety degrees, so they don't have direct eye contact. George introduces everyone by first names, and asks if they could use these names, when they talk about each other, rather than 'he' or 'she'.

Both parties are given uninterrupted time to put their case. This is when one party speaks first, and the other has to grin and bear it, without speaking. They can make notes. This is often the hardest part, because to be able to listen to a litany of complaints in silence without reacting is near impossible. George includes in his list 'huffing and puffing, raised eyebrows and other aggressive gestures.'

Jo is first to start. She has only one thing on her mind, and before two sentences are out, she is in tears again.

'It's the dog,' she says, 'I can hear it whining and barking at all hours. And when I heard him throwing the dog across the room I was so upset.'

'You mean Harry?' asks George.

Harry looks at Teresa and sees fire in her eyes.

'Yes, and he keeps shouting at the dog, and we can hear everything he says, and I can't stand it. That's not how we treat our dog.'

Teresa rolls her eyes, folds her arms, and partially turns away from Jo.

'Tell us how you treat your dog, Jo.' Sarah adds gently.

'Well, with respect! You know, we don't have to shout at it, and Harry takes her out for walks, because that's something I can't do. So, she dont get restless being stuck in all the time.'

Peter comes in at last. 'And it's that and all the noise, the banging of doors, and the shouting.'

George sums up the story after getting details of when the noises are happening, and how it is making them feel. He thanks the other couple for being patient and waiting without comment, although he knows that by body language alone, they have made their feelings plain. Then he invites them to begin.

Teresa launches in with 'I don't know what this lady is on about noise. We don't deliberately make noise, only what most normal folk do every day, like washing up, going to't toilet, cooking and such. Anyone would think we were banging doors on purpose, but why would anyone do that I'd like to know? And as for 't dog, we had RSPCA round and they said there were nowt wrong wi 't dog that they could see.'

Harry adds his two pennorth. 'I'm not a cruel man. I love my dog, and that story about me chuckin' it across room like she says is just not true. And anyway, what about their dog? We can hear that as well you know, and we don't complain about that do we?'

For small quiet man Harry is getting quite het up, and all of a sudden Peter stands up, saying 'I'm not staying here to listen to this. I've had enough!' And visibly shaking he makes his way to the door.

George has to act quickly, and without consulting his partner gets up to follow Peter, trusting that Sarah will know what to do in his absence. He finds Peter standing in the corridor, shaking and almost in tears. This is the most emotion he has had to deal with in a long time, in a buttoned-down small life, and he is not fully in control of himself.

'Peter – please don't go. If you go now when everything is in this state of high arousal, it will make the situation worse. We can't leave it like this. I know how this situation is making you both feel, and that's why we agreed to come here today, because I'm sure neither of you wants this to continue. Do you?'

Peter stands there, still shaking, and it is a while before he can take control of his voice. He looks ill.

'I… you see… I… I lost my wife – last year. Cancer. She was like, everything to me, and I've not been well myself since then.' There are tears in his eyes.' Its having Jo to look after that's keeping me going, stops me brooding over it. Jo and the dog, like. You know what I mean. And it's the stress of all this stuff, and the noise. I'm thinking of moving back to Barnsley. I wish I'd never left there.'

George lets it all flow, knowing that letting it all out is better than keeping it all in. He stands silent for a minute. But then the door opens and Jo comes out and touches Peter's arm.

'Look love,' she says, 'I don't want to be here either. But I don't want this trouble to go on any more. We've tried council and police and nothing got any better. I hate all this, but if we don't stay its gonna get worse, and I can't stand any more.'

'She's right, you know Peter,' says George. 'I know it's difficult, but this is your best chance of putting it right. I tell you what we'll do. You go to your room for a few minutes and Sarah and I will call you in a bit. Make yourself some tea or coffee in the kitchen, OK.'

*

Sarah by this time has moved the other couple into their separate room.

'How about,' says George,' if we get the two women together first and then the two men? What do you think?'

'You're right,' she says. 'It's probably the fear of Harry that's making it worse for Jo. And when she's upset, Peter's upset. Let's give it a go.'

*

The two women sit without looking at each other.

'Jo,' says Sarah. 'I am guessing, but I feel this is not just about dogs, is it? Am I right?'

Jo's tears start to flow again.

'No.' She whispers, her eyes on the table.

'Would you like to tell us, Jo? Take your time.'

'It's him. Its Harry. I'm scared of him. When he shouts, I get frightened.'

'Why is that, Jo?'

'You see. The way I am now. I wasn't always like this. It was my husband, he was violent. Very violent. He used to hit me, beat me up. And one day he threw me down, and I hurt me back. I had to go to hospital. And since then, I can't stand up for long, and I can't walk far. He ruined my life. And I… I can't stand it when I hear Harry shouting. I can't bear it. And all I have now is my cousin Peter, and he's a bit of a wreck too, since he lost his wife, you know. We're like two lonely people, with no-one to talk to. And he's not much of a talker. Just him and his dog like.'

George and Sarah just sit and let the silence flow for a minute. Then George looks at Teresa, who has by now turned her body towards Jo, and her look has changed from contempt to horror.

'Jo. I'm so sorry. I didn't know. If I'd known all this…'

'Teresa,' George begins slowly. 'What would you say is Jo's greatest need?'

'If it were me… I don't know… if it were me, I suppose I'd want another woman to talk to.'

'I think you're right there Teresa. It's not really about the dog is it. Could you be that other woman, do you think?'

Teresa slowly lets the penny drop.

'You know, love, what upsets us the most is them letters from council, and police comin' round. I don't mind if you've got a problem really, but where we were before people used to come and talk to us, and we'd sort it out, like.'

'But I can't walk up them stairs, Teresa.'

'No, love. I understand. What about if you write a note and ask Peter to stick it through our door?'

'I could do that, I suppose,' Jo is not too happy with that.

'Is there something more you could do, as a neighbour,' Sarah ventures with a smile.

'What about,' and slowly Teresa is beginning to unravel. 'What about if I were to come down and see you from time to time? Would you like that?'

And at this point Jo's tears start to flow again, and she nods her head and even smiles. 'Yes, yes. I would like that. Thank you.'

*

'Tell me about your dog, Harry.'

George begins the conversation with the two men.

'It's a Staffy, like I said.'

'A Staffordshire Terrier?'

'Aye. And they're good little hunters like, and a bit lively.'

'So, are you just as lively with him?'

Harry grins. 'Yeah. You have to be. We have a lot o' fun, like'

'In the flat?'

'Yeah. And down at me house where I do me caring. They like him as well. He sort o' cheers 'em up, like.'

'So maybe some of this fun you're talking about is what causes the noise that Jo is talking about?'

'Yeah, probably'

'And what about your dog, Peter?'

Peter's story is not so full of fun. He has a mongrel of a quiet temperament. They chat about that for a few minutes.

'Have the dogs ever met?' asks George with a smile.

'No,' says Peter.

'Do you think they might be friends, Harry?'

'Well, you don't know till you try, do yer?' Harry looks quizzically at Peter.

'Wanna try it?'

'Oh, I… er…' Peter hesitates. This might be one step outside his comfort zone.

'I think that might be a peace offering from Harry, Peter. What do you think?'

'We could go for a pint if yer like, 'says Harry.

'Oh, I don't know. I don't go to pubs that much.'

'There's the Crown and Sceptre just down the road,' says Harry, 'They don't mind dogs.'

'Peter? It would get you out of the flat for a bit, wouldn't it?' George is pushing gently.

'All right then. I don't mind if I do.' Peter almost smiles. He is taking a chance on this little man who he doesn't really know at all.

'Great!' says George. 'Shall we put that on your agreement?'

The agreement mentions some simple things Harry can do to insulate the door frames in their flat to stop them banging, Teresa knocking on Jo's door, and Harry and Peter going for a pint.

'Sounds simple, doesn't it,' George says to Sarah afterwards.

'But it doesn't tell the whole story, does it.'

'How are you feeling love?' Sarah asks.

'I think I could do with a pint meself, how about you?'

'And a hug?'

'And a hug!'

The last sunrise

There was no sunrise. It was as if the sun had decided to join the rest of the townsfolk in these strange, suspended days between Christmas and New Year, and just stay in bed. Following a pinkish sliver of colour between the horizon and the blanket of cloud, the day merely lightened its overall grey a shade or two.

Simon left the curtains open and allowed the room's shadows to merge with those outside. Slowly the still and shrunken form of his Annie would begin to take shape amid the grey dunes of the crumpled bedding. Shivering and stretching his aching body, he slipped on his dressing gown and silently padded downstairs to make tea.

'Annie... tea.'

He began to straighten the quilt and the under sheet around her. Not that there had been much disturbance, for even though she hardly slept, neither was she fully awake in the night, and had not energy enough to toss and turn in her pain. Tenderly he lifted her, enfolded her, while he raised the pillows. So little left of her. He took her soft brush and gently straightened her remaining hair, kissed her forehead.

Annie's eyes opened. They creased in a smile as he leaned over to reach her teacup, and as his face came level again with her's he was surprised as he always was by the light that shone from them. His moment of sunrise. And as ever, his grimly set face crumpled into the lopsided grin that she always inspired, and cherished. They shared a moment of wordless greeting.

In that moment they surveyed one another. For some years now each had been able to assess the other's mood and health just by a look and a gesture, a passing subliminal activity, unseen by younger folk who occasionally paid their obligatory calls. His eyes would say – How are you today? Oh, I'm sorry. I'll get you something for it. Hold on love. Soon be better. I'm here. Hold on.

Today there was a shade less Annie, a shade more the enemy. The unseen but much felt presence waiting by the bed. He had taken her voice a while ago, and most of her body. But the real Annie still filled the house, quietly refusing to leave until she was ready.

Annie's eyes took in the careworn features of her man. She knew he was not sleeping but fitfully. He tried not to be too restless by her side, and when he could not stay still any longer, he crept about the house, made tea, listened to the radio, wrote things down, (she had an idea what they were), and tried to re-enter the bed without disturbing her. All of which she heard in every detail, for the small hours reveal everything to the unsleeping.

And his cold hand would find its customary way across the sheet to touch her thigh and stroke it, and sometimes clasp her hand, a fleshless bunch of twigs. Such was her pain that he was no longer able to roll over and hold her body to his. Both ebbed and flowed in sleep, both knew when the other was awake. These were the times of silent communion in the endless hours, a language that only the old understand, that is beyond the imagination of children.

Simon helped her to sup her tea with a practised hand, entwining her fingers around cup and handle, when it was not too hot, and raising it to her lips, so as to keep the illusion that she was still able to do it herself, while the other hand kept a bundle of tissues beneath her lip. He would not have her shamed by soiled bedding. In between sips he got her to swallow the right number of pills from the collection in the drawer. He was an orderly man. She was once an efficient and busy woman, in a loving, not a bustling way. Even now there was decorum. It was part of his service to her.

After some warm porridge oats, he took her methodically through the routines of the bedpan, the bed bath and the cleaning of teeth, all of which he did with the utmost tenderness, knowing what a torture they were to her. Then he saw to his own needs, bringing the paper for her to read the while.

At about the expected time, he saw through the kitchen window the doctor's car approaching, and went to unfasten the door, leaving it slightly ajar. As the slight figure entered, warmly coated and with bag in hand, she looked up into his face, noting the increasing dark shadows beneath his eyes.

'Simon?'

With the one word she asked several questions.

Simon smiled and shook his head.

'She's all ready for you, Doctor.'

'Hello, Annie.' Doctor Pearce entered the bedroom, taking in the waxen figure propped against pillows, the tidy bed, the cheerful bedside light, the magazines, and papers. She was grateful for Simon. She sensed what went on in this room, in this house. She smiled her response to it as she took Annie's hand and squeezed it. Annie's eyes shone, and they flashed a little glance at her lover, who stood in the doorway, clasping his hands across his chest.

Without hurry, almost casually, the doctor carried out her usual tests, pulse, blood pressure, eyes, reflexes, before giving her the injection. All the while chatting to Annie in a jokey way, about the weather, the colds, the hangovers of the season, in a manner which somehow made allowances for the fact that the patient could not respond, and yet assumed that responses had been made. Simon admired the performance. He had learned from it in the last few months.

'Simon,' After, in the kitchen, 'I think it might be today.' She looked at his face and saw nothing but calm.

'I think so too,' he said. 'She's ready.'

'Are *you* ready, Simon?'

'Aye, love, I am.'

'Is there anybody you'd like us to contact?'

'Please.'

He took a small envelope from his pocket and gave it to her. She was not surprised. She knew he would have it organised, even though he might not be able to do it himself.

'I'll leave you this.' She gave him a small bottle of liquid. 'In case it gets more than she can bear. All right?'

'All right.' They exchanged a heavy glance, and the doctor emitted a long weary sigh, before she left the house without saying goodbye.

Simon put the kettle on, and meanwhile set about washing up the few breakfast things. With another two cups on a tray, he climbed the stairs, but stopped halfway up, listening. There was nothing to hear, but he knew she had just called him. There was a different kind of silence.

Entering the room he found her not in repose, but off the pillows, her little body stretched across the quilt, with one arm reaching towards the door. He felt a sharp crack of alarm grip his chest, and hastily laid the tea tray on the floor, not without some spillage.

'Annie! Oh, my little Annie!'

He gathered her up in his arms and heedless of her condition clasped her to him and lay back on the pillows. Her eyes were open and full of tears, as she looked into his. They said to him, 'I wanted you to be here. You nearly missed it.'

She was panting, very shallow. In just moments, the panting ceased, and a faint rasp left her throat.

He did not move until long afterwards. He held her until there was no warmth left, then gently arranged her amid the pillows. He tidied the bed. Took the tea tray downstairs.

What he did next was part of a plan he had sorted in his

long night-time vigils. He put out the empties and left a note for the milkman. He left the kitchen door on the latch. He went right round the house, emptying bins, sorting out washing, and did the few remaining bits of ironing.

He turned off the heating. Then he went to a drawer in the sideboard and took out a handful of letters. Each was sealed and addressed. Some were stamped. Some just had single names on. One was to his sister. Two were for his sons. These he took upstairs.

He went to the toilet. Then he opened his wardrobe, and took out two full bottles of pain killers, and a large full bottle of whisky. He also had the bottle the doctor had given him today.

He brought a reclining armchair alongside the bed, placed his bottles on the bedside table. He left his letters there too. Then he picked up the phone, and rang the doctor's surgery, to tell them about Annie. He told them he was fine, and they need not rush. This afternoon would do.

He sat in the armchair, and looked at the figure of Annie, now so beautiful in peace. He opened the bottles. First, he took the doctor's morphine, then the pills, two or three at a time, washed down with whisky.

'See you soon, love.'

He remembered to turn off the light, so that his sons would not have too big a bill to pay. The greyness of the day merged once more with the greyness of the room. The sun, never having risen, neither did it set. The day just faded away.

Aftermath

Late on a grey afternoon in December Doctor Sarah Lane pulled up outside the house of one of her long-term patients. She knew why she was here. The husband had called earlier in the day to say his wife was dead. That morning as she left his house, she had told him it would probably be today. He seemed to know, and when she left him, he was calm, and accepting. He had given her some documents to distribute in the event.

As was her habit, she knocked on the kitchen door and let herself in, knowing that he would be upstairs with his wife.

'Simon?' She called.

No answer. This was unusual. Simon was a punctilious caring man, very well organised. She called again, a bit louder. Into the living room. Everything neatly arranged. No sound. She turned on the lights, and quietly made her way up the stairs.

'Simon, its me.' No response. She looked toward the bathroom. No-one in there, the door was open. She gently pushed open the door of the bedroom.

As a doctor she was trained in calm ways, used to unpleasant and often alarming situations. Here she was expecting the usual calm and methodical man going about the business of caring for his dying wife. Expecting death, but not this.

The wife was laid out neatly in the bed as if by an undertaker. There was hardly any flesh left on her body, but her hair was combed and she looked at peace. One hand lay across her stomach. The other was entwined in the hand of her husband, who sat in the chair by her side, his chin resting on his chest, eyes closed.

Beside him on the bedside chest, an empty bottle of whisky, some empty medicine bottles, and the one she had given him this morning, for his wife.

'Simon…' But she already knew.

She touched his forehead. Cold. She felt his neck pulse. None.

'Oh Simon! No, no, no!'

She felt the need to sit, and lowered herself onto the bed. She took out of her case the papers Simon had given her this morning. It gave her the names of his two sons. She wondered at the time why he would do this. Now she took out her phone and dialled one of the numbers.

While she waited, she noticed among the other numbers that of an undertaker, and a catholic priest. There was a small pile of letters by the bedside. No-one was answering her call, so she glanced at the letters. Two were for Simon's sons, two or three more bore the names of what she guessed must be a priest and an undertaker. There was only an answer phone message, so she left a message asking the son to come to the house with his brother that evening. She would see them at seven and explain what had happened.

Leaving the lights on, she slowly went downstairs, and left the house, left the latch on the kitchen door locked this time, which Simon had left unlocked for her. She called her surgery and told them she was not returning till tomorrow, and went home.

*

She waited outside the house just before seven, and in a few minutes two cars drew up and two men got out. As they walked down the driveway, she intercepted them.

'I'm Dr Sarah Lane. I have been looking after your mother.'

'Why are you here then, and where's my dad?' Robert was not as polite as his father.

'Yeah, where's our dad?' said David. 'What's going on?'

'Look, before you go in,' she said, as calmly as she could, 'you need to know…'

'Need to know what?' Robert was getting annoyed.

'I was here this morning, and your dad and I discussed the situation. He knew that your mother might die today.'

'Well why didn't he bloody ring us then? Where is he?'

'I'm afraid he couldn't. You see, both your parents are dead. I'm really sorry to shock you, but there are rules about what we're allowed to tell people on the phone. That's why I asked you to come tonight.'

Sarah herself was on the verge of tears. She felt as bad

about it as they did, and had regarded Simon as a friend. 'Can we go in please?'

'Jesus Christ!' Robert was angry, and disbelieving. 'Why didn't someone tell us earlier?' He fiddled with some keys and let them all in to the kitchen.

'I called you at four Robert, but your phone just gave me a recorded message. Look, make your way upstairs and we'll talk a bit later.'

The two men looked angrily at her, but then left her in the kitchen and went up the stairs. She found the kettle and began making some coffee. It was some time before they returned, very subdued. She offered them some coffee, and they sat silently round the table. Robert put the letters down in front of them. He also showed her the empty bottles that he had brought from upstairs.

'Is this your doing?' he said accusingly.

'Not exactly, no,' she said. 'Let me explain.'

David the younger brother, sat speechless with tears in his eyes.

'I think you've got a lot of explaining to do, Doctor. You've kept us in the dark over this!'

'Look,' she said, somehow getting back into her dispassionate doctorly manner. 'Your father was a well organised, very caring man. I relied on him a great deal in looking after your mother. I always knew he would do the right thing, unlike many other of my patients.'

'Is this what you call the right thing then? Bloody suicide? He were as fit as a fiddle, our Dad.'

'Yes, I know he was. I am as shocked as you are over what's happened. Look, the liquid in this bottle was what

I gave him to give to your mother if her pain became unbearable. The whisky, the other pills, I knew nothing about that, believe me.'

'Look Robert' David spoke through a shaky voice. 'Get off your high horse and have a bit of respect. There's two dead parents upstairs, and there's no call for you to go shouting at the doctor like that.'

Turning to Sarah, he went on, 'I'm sorry Doc, it's just that…'

'I know David, it's all right. This is an unprecedented situation. I'm finding it hard to understand myself. Your father gave no indication of what he intended to do. There will have to be an inquest. I think your best thing now is to go home, talk to your families, get in touch with the undertakers, and I think if you open those letters, your father will have left you some instructions, if I know him. At times like this we need to get organised, do what has to be done, and let things take their course. I know you will all be very shocked, but out of respect for your parents, get cracking, and deal with the emotional side of it later. Do you think you can do that?'

*

An envelope labelled 'Undertakers'

> *Don't worry, sons, I am not letting these bastards take you for a ride (only me and Annie!) Here are two funeral plans I set up some years ago. You won't have to pay for anything.*

Our ashes – when you feel ready for it, sprinkle us into the river Colne, or any river that flows into the North sea. That's where I came from. Don't for god's sake stick us on the mantelpiece. And you won't have to bother visiting any gravestones. What remains of us will be in your heads and your hearts. OK?

Dad

*

Message for Father Donald

Annie was a devout Catholic. I was not. I was a humanist. Out of respect for her I will allow you to do whatever it is you do at your church. I respected her religion, but I could never go in for all that mumbo jumbo myself. Our love was so strong that these things did not matter. I doubt if my sons will want two funerals, so I suggest you go to the crematorium service to which I have invited a humanist speaker. Then you can say a mass for her at your place. Thanks for your care for her. Simon.

Attached to this, a poem. 'Feed it', in which Simon posed the idea that god is just that – an idea. Robert and David were also challenged by this idea, and grew up with no religion, Annie not being their own mother. They wondered how their dad could have lived with this during his long second marriage, something he never talked about. Something they now begin to question. Who was he? Did they really know him?

*

Another envelope labelled 'PC. Small bedroom. 126'

Robert and David sat squashed awkwardly in the small bedroom, their father's study. There was a desk, which spanned the width of the small room, a computer, printer and various electronic odds and ends, lots of ring binders, each carefully labelled, Instructions, Guarantees, Legal, some with the names of organisations their dad worked for, and one with just a pound sign, containing all his neatly documented financial affairs. There were containers of batteries, plugs, rubber bands and staples, hearing aids.

'I didn't know he wore hearing aids, did you?' Robert asked.

David, who was partially hearing himself, said no. 'What's this PC thing supposed to mean?'

They spent some time minutely examining all these folders, and getting nowhere. Then David, leaning back in his father's reclining chair looked up at a shelf overhead. Underneath the shelf was a label – 'Poet's corner'.

'PC – Poet's corner! That might be it.' They stood up, and there were a dozen folders, each with a label on them, 1-100, 101-200, etc. Taking down the second of these, 101-200, David opened it at no. 126. A poem called 'Baptism'

'You were a black baby,' he read. It went on to describe the shock of being presented with a child starved of oxygen in the womb, and who is baptized in the incubator by a priest, 'who welcomed you to earth and heaven alike, in case you should leave too soon.'

'Who's he writing about? A black baby? Did he have an affair with a black woman?'

'No,' said Robert. 'This must have been you. I was three when you were born, and I vaguely remember seeing you in a glass box in the hospital. They kept you in for weeks. Me mum said something about it.'

David read it again to himself. There were tears in his eyes. It was a love poem to a child.

*

A little note fell out of the page behind the poem. It said 'PC 247'.

Robert went to the next folder, and found 247. It was called 'Debut 1' and next to it was 'Debut 2'. They described their father's joy and fear at becoming a grandfather. Robert's first daughter was also seriously ill at birth, and spent months in an incubator.

'A cuddle, a shriek of laughter, a suck of a warm wet breast, all that is needed to get things started'

And when she was finally released, he is invited to hold her for the first time.

'That first kiss, on the soft downy skull, is all I can manage in lieue of words, sealing the bond, closing the circle.'

'I never knew,' said Robert, deeply moved for all his cynicism, 'he was writing about us all the time, did you? He never said.' He it was who had inherited the down to earth practical side of his father, and who rarely showed his feelings.

Another note fell out of the folder. 'Letter three. Microwave.' In the microwave, another bundle of letters. One was addressed to 'Your mum'

'Oh no! I'm not having this!'

Robert's mother was abandoned by his father for the woman on the bed upstairs twenty-five years ago. He was seventeen at the time, and took it very badly. They had become reconciled over the years, up to a point, but Robert and David had always guarded their mother from contact with Simon. Robert began to rip open the envelope.

'Robert – wait!' David grabbed the envelope from his brother. But it was already opened. Another envelope fell out, and a handwritten note as well as an old photograph.

'A-a-a!' it said. 'Not so hasty. This is a private matter between me and your mum. Let her have it.'

The picture showed a young couple in their twenties. It looked as if it was the 1970s, as the man had a flowered shirt and flared trousers, and a great deal of shoulder length hair. The woman had flowers in her copious hair and she was clinging onto the man in a passionate embrace.

'Bloody hell! Look at this,' said David. His dad had been bald for as long as he could remember, as was Robert since his twenties. 'This must be them. Don't they look daft!'

'Yeah,' said Robert, 'but that's where you and me came from.'

The continuous sequence of notes and letters and poems was making Robert very uneasy, as if Simon was talking to them all over the house, which he was in fact. Although their contact was infrequent, Simon knew his sons better than they knew him.

'Robert. Look there's time for this later. We need to get the undertaker sorted, and we have to tell the kids what's happened. Leave it now, and let's go.'

'I don't want the old sod upsetting our mum all over again,' Robert said, full of anger and the memory of the shock of his dad's leaving. But he left the envelope with David, and they turned off all the lights, except for one to deter burglars, and made their way separately to their own homes, to break the bad news.

*

The news of the death of two grandparents at once was not such a shock to the children as Robert and David had imagined. They knew that Annie was going to die, although what that actually meant was hard for them to understand. This woman who they had seen on her bed once or twice in the last few months had not been able to speak to them for some time. Their parents had kept the visits brief, so as not to upset them. And contact with them was pretty infrequent anyway, ever since the split had put some distance between the sons and their dad and his new wife. Their own children were busy all the time with school events, sports and drama, so Simon and his wife were not as well known to them as the various other grandparents, who were all still living.

So, life went on pretty much as usual for the next few

days, as the two brothers organised the removal of the bodies and tried to set up a funeral. But after two days some letters arrived addressed to the children, and one each for Robert and David. This was unusual in the age of social media. The five grandchildren all used phones and tablets to communicate with their friends and each other. None of them had ever received a letter in their short lives.

Each child had a personal letter from Simon, which showed them that he knew them much better than they knew him. Young children do not know a great deal about the adults in their lives as people. That comes later, and sometimes too late. Each one had an invitation to visit his house and an instruction to look for various places in the house. It was not long till Christmas, and the children were pretty hyped up already. So, they nagged Robert and David to take them to the house immediately. They all turned up at once the same evening.

In the airing cupboard, the bathroom cabinet, under Simon's desk, beneath a pillow in one of the bedrooms and behind the TV they each found a parcel with their name on it, and a label that said 'Not to be opened until Christmas day!' But they also read on each label a different reference number, beginning with PC. There was also a cache of parcels for the adults in a bag in the garage. Another envelope was addressed to the whole family. Robert opened this one, and found a set of tickets for all of them to attend the local pantomime.

He wondered how Simon had ever found the time to organise all this while looking after his dying wife. But then he remembered. His Dad, despite his age, was a well organised man like himself. He knew his way around a computer. He had bought all this stuff online. He must have been planning his own death for some months beforehand.

There followed a small pantomime as the two dads pretended not to know what the PC numbers meant. It was not long before Jack, the oldest boy, figured it out. They grabbed all the folders of poetry and spread them out on the floor. Each child found a poem that had a particular bearing on them.

They were magical, mocking, fantastical, funny and plain daft, and soon they were all giggling and sharing their poems. The one that struck a chord with all of them was 'Uncle Beverley', in which a mischievous and magical uncle held a party for the children, involving electric spaghetti which joined them all together round the table.

Down our noses came a stream
Of multi-coloured snotty steam,
A prickling down our backs and bums
And sparks between our fingers and thumbs.

The two Dads joined in the fun, which took their minds off the awful task they had before them.

*

At the post mortem, all the adults waited for the coroner to sum up his findings. In the case of Annie, it was straightforward. The doctor had given a summary of her gradual decline and succumbing to lung cancer.

For Simon, she was made to sit through a lengthy cross examination. She explained how she had attended to his needs in looking after his wife over several months, and had no knowledge of his intentions. On the last day she had given him a bottle of morphine to ease her pain, knowing that it might be her last day.

'But there is more to it than that Doctor Lane, is there not?' asked the coroner.

'Yes sir, Simon himself had a condition from which he knew he would not recover. He wished it to be kept secret from his family.'

'But this was not the cause of his death, doctor?'

'No, it would have been several months later, and probably as painful as his wife's condition.'

This was news to Robert and David, who sat stony faced trying to take it all in.

After the verdict of suicide, as they all left the court, they approached the doctor.

'What was this condition, doctor? How come we didn't know?'

She looked at their serious faces, both of them now subdued and on the verge of tears.

'Simon was a remarkable man you know. He had complete control over his situation, and I trusted him to do the right thing by his wife. He asked me not to say anything to you about his illness. And, you know, we have to abide by our professional rules. He asked me to give you this. I think it will tell you all you need to know.'

She handed them a letter. They shook hands and parted.

David and Robert made their way to a nearby pub, sat down with a pint each, and opened the letter.

Dear Robert and David,

I have asked Doctor Lane to give you this after the post mortem. She has been a great support to me and Annie, and I hope you will respect her for her professional integrity. There is nothing underhand about what she has done. It was all down to me.

First of all, I want you to know that I bear no ill will to your mother, who was a great wife and mother, and treated me well. I have sent her a letter as well. When we married it was in haste, as I was offered a job in another part of the country soon after we had met, which was too good to turn down. I either had to leave her behind or we went together. In those days people got married rather than living together.

But I was so immature and inexperienced. My upbringing was poor and I had only one girlfriend before her. So, I knew nothing about how to love a woman and treat her with respect. I was like her child.

We stayed together nevertheless, and had you two. We moved around the country quite a bit. But I slowly became aware that I had missed so much of growing up, and had not had time to find out who I really was and what I really needed. It was when I did the Open University that we began to drift apart. Meeting so many other people in the same situation made me see what I had been missing as a young man.

This led to a change of career and your mum. bless her, helped us to save up, and reorganise so that I could go away to train as a teacher. Working with lots of parents with disabled children brought me into contact with many women in difficult situations. That is how I met Annie. She was like a lightning bolt to me, and I was smitten from the first time we met. We had to work together over many months, and I knew she was the woman I wanted to devote the rest of my life to.

So, I did that thing which split us all apart. I knew what a hurtful thing I was doing, but my love for Annie was so strong it drove me on.

I know there has been an unspoken but potent rift between us since then, which has caused there to be some distance between us. But you have become more like friends to me than sons. Since we came together again, I have come to love the kids as much as you do, and I wish we could have spent more time together.

As you know I have tried always to treat you with respect. I decided long ago not to criticise anything you did, but to praise where praise is due. I am very proud of you both and all your children. You have become great Dads, and you are lucky to have such great wives. I love you both more than I can say.

However, as you will now know, it wasn't just Annie that was ill. A few months ago, I was diagnosed with pancreatic cancer. This is incurable and very painful. I asked Dr Lane to keep it quiet. I would have succumbed within about nine months. Seeing the desperate time that Annie was having, I did not want you to have to go through it all again. And neither did I think I could cope with being alone without Annie.

And so, Robert, this old sod won't be troubling you any more after a few days. If you find yourself wondering who I really was my autobiography is in my poems. I stopped writing diaries many years ago, and those I had written I destroyed a few weeks ago. There is a record of all the jobs I had, and an album of affirmations from the people I worked for in resolving their conflicts.

Should you decide to publish any of my poems you will find that task infinitely more difficult than disposing of two elderly relatives, but in the end, much more rewarding. Good luck with that.

Goodbye my sons,

May you never have to suffer so much again,

Dad

Zoe the wrestler

'What do you like about school?'
'Nothing.'

Zoe's response to his pre-mediation questionnaire makes George smile. This one's going to be fun, he thinks.

Having driven for an hour and a half his phone rings while on the motorway. He picks it up on his arrival at the school.

'This mediation is cancelled. The LA rep says she has already made the decision to allow an assessment of Zoe, so you don't need to meet.'

George gratefully settles down with the cup of tea offered by the school secretary, and goes to the next message.

'Please ignore last message. Parent wants to go ahead anyway. Not happy with school.'

'Ah, good,' thinks George, 'so let battle commence.'

*

Something is rotten in the state of Denmark. For a start the

LA officer is far too young and pretty to be bearing all this responsibility. Her boss has been unable to make it, and she has no sign of any wrinkles or grey hairs. The school special needs teacher is also on loan from another school, as the present one is off sick. The parent has a face like thunder, and is supported by a formidable woman from a company called 'Harmony' who looks as if she will take no nonsense. The two of them begin talking about the case before George has even had time to welcome everyone.

'We're here because Mum is sick and tired of all the trouble this school is causing for her Zoe.' Harmony's opening line is swiftly reinforced by Mum, who goes on with, 'Zoe was sick last night when she got home, and went straight to her room. She said she was bullied again by them two girls and she was kept in isolation for two hours.'

George raises his hands in a 'Whooooaa' sort of gesture, and says 'Er, before we begin how about we introduce ourselves, and then I will tell you how mediation works.'

He goes through the routines in a gentle but assertive manner, which while sounding calm and reassuring also leaves the impression that he is in charge and there will be order. This is reinforced by a few minutes of papers being handed round and signed, which results in everyone having agreed to behave themselves whatever feelings are boiling up inside. He catches the eye of Mary, the young Local Authority officer, in a look that says 'Don't worry love, it'll be all right.' And she smiles faintly.

'So, Jane,' to the parent, 'tell me about Zoe. I believe she has a diagnosis of ASD?'

'Aye, and Tourette's, as well. She keeps making them

noises and swearing. That's what annoys all the other kids and the teachers.'

'Does she actually have a diagnosis though?'

'It's PDA as well,' the Harmony woman, Ann butts in.

'Hang on a minute,' says George, 'Pathological Demand Avoidance? Is this diagnosed as well?'

Ann goes on. 'Whatever they ask her to do she refuses to do it.'

'And that's what gets her into trouble,' says Jane. 'She's the same at home, only different if you know what I mean.'

'No Jane, I don't. Tell me what is different at home.'

'Well, she don't have to do any school work, so that's a blessing, 'cos she wouldn't do it if they gave it her. But if I ask her to do something she will automatically refuse to do it.'

'Such as?' George gently probes.

'Like getting washed, or going to bed, or cleaning up after herself.'

'So does she do any of those at all?'

'Only when she decides to do them.'

'You mean she likes to be in control?'

'That's it. You get used to it after a while.'

'These noises you mentioned, does she do those at home?'

'Oh, tell me about it! She whistles, she hums, she swears. I have to tell her to shut up sometimes, 'cos she don't know she's doing it, like in the middle of a TV programme.'

'Is there any pattern to it that you can recognise?'

'It's when she's stressed,' Ann butts in, 'or thinking over stuff that's happened at school. And she don't like noise, and she don't like quiet either.'

Jane goes on. 'The only time she stops completely is when she's wrestling.'

'Wrestling?' says George, trying to imagine a girl wrestling with her mum while whistling, humming and swearing.

'Aye, she goes to a wrestling club. She likes that. It makes her calm down when she's fighting and throwing people round the place, know what I mean?'

Jane shows no sign of humour. George catches the eye of Mary again, who is trying not to grin.

'My other two daughters when they come round, they usually grab hold of her and they have a bit of a go, it's like her way of saying hello, you see.'

'What an interesting family,' says George, and immediately wishes he hadn't said that. Ann and Jane scowl at him.

'Tell me what happens at school, then.'

'Well,' says Jane, with an air of determination. 'Well for a start she's not in normal lessons. They keep her out most of the time. The teachers can't cope with her making all them noises, and the other kids keep telling her to shut up. And if she don't like what they're teaching she won't do it.'

George is beginning to warm to this feisty young woman.

'When you say, not in normal lessons, where is she then?'

'She's with a little group of kids who can't read and write and think as fast as the others. And that's what bothers her, 'cos she's very bright, and she can't cope with everything being so slow. So that ups her stress levels and she starts whistling and swearing even more.'

'So, it's like, she gets put in isolation' says Ann, 'for disturbing the other kids. So, she's not learning anything at all. Because even if they give her some work to do, she'll refuse to do it.'

'You mentioned a minute ago her not liking noise or quiet,' says George.

'That's right,' Mum continues. 'She gets stressed at the noise of changing lessons, and play time. But she can't cope with it being too quiet either. That's when she makes more noises.'

'So, I imagine the other children find this hard to understand?' asks George.

'That's right. She gets bullied a lot,' says Mum. 'Two girls in particular, they're always on at her, so staff have to cope with that as well. And on top of all that they keep telling her off for making noises.'

Ann goes on. 'And she says she's only doing maths and English, so she's bored, poor lass.'

Helen the SENCO* comes in at this point, having been made to listen to this tirade of unhappiness for so long.

'I'm sorry but that's just not true.'

George thanks the two women who have held the floor and raised the temperature considerably.

'I'd like to come to Helen now. How would you respond to what you have heard so far?'

'First of all, can I say I've only been here for a few weeks, as I'm covering for the school SENCO who is on long-term

---

* Special educational needs coordinator

sick. So, I'm only just beginning to get to know Zoe, although she does take up a lot of my time.'

'Do you get on with her, would you say,' asks George, hoping that this gentle woman has found another side of this difficult girl.

'Fortunately, yes, since I don't have to teach her directly. We mostly just talk, you see. But let me show you this.'

She unfolds a document. 'This is Zoe's timetable. She is doing most of the subjects on the curriculum. I think she may call it English because most of the lessons involve some writing. And maybe she ignores the stuff that she doesn't like. But she does do music, art, and PE. She is with the small groups because the teachers find her difficult to manage in large classes, as she disrupts the work of the other children. And she does have some down time on her own, when things get stressful for her.'

'What about friends?' asks George, knowing the answer already.

'Zoe doesn't have any real friends, I'm afraid. She would say she has two or three that she likes, but I don't think she knows what it means to be a friend.'

'Going back to our earlier conversation, she does have a diagnosis of ASD, I believe. But what about the other conditions that Jane mentioned?'

'At the moment we have nothing in writing about that. But I believe, am I right, that she has another appointment with the paediatrician soon?'

'In a couple of weeks yes,' says Mum.

George presses on. 'And have you or the staff had any specific training in dealing with children with ASD?'

'I have,' says Helen, 'but I am not sure about the staff as a whole.'

Ann jumps in here. 'If they had they wouldn't be treating her the way they do, love. They treat her like a naughty girl all the time, and keep telling her off for swearing, when she can't help it. Do you think any normal girl would talk like that? Why can't they just ignore it?'

'Maybe,' says Helen, 'they're worried about the effect on the other children.'

Jane is getting more wound up at this point. 'And me, I don't get to hear about what's going on most of the time. In the last two years I've only spoken to any staff a couple of times. And that's only when something's wrong. I have to ask Zoe what's been going on, and she's always so upset she can't tell me.'

George feels the need to take the heat out of things.

'Perhaps we can talk about how school communicates with Mum later. Can I bring in Mary now.' Turning to the LA woman who has sat patiently though all the turmoil. 'I believe you have said that you will go ahead now and recommend that Zoe is assessed by the LA?'

Mary smiles at last. 'Yes. We had an application about two months ago from Helen. And I've decided to recommend an assessment. But I don't think it mentioned all of the conditions we have heard about today. Could you bring me up to date please, Helen?'

Helen agrees to incorporate recent information and to bring in extra material from the Educational Psychologist and the paediatric report which is soon to take place.

George quickly moves to get them to agree a timetable

for these actions.

'Now,' he goes on,' I know Zoe is only here until the end of the summer term. From what you have heard, Mary and Helen, do you foresee Zoe being able to move on to a local high school in September.'

Ann butts in again. 'She is not going to be able to cope with a big high school. Don't you think, Jane?'

'No, you're right there. And I don't think I can cope with the prospect of her coming home every day even more stressed. I'm already at the limit of what I can handle. I can't see how all them teachers are ever going to understand our Zoe, or wanting to talk to me about her.'

George begins a conversation with Mary and Helen about local special schools. There are none that deal with high functioning children like Zoe. But there are two that deal with autism. Jane agrees to visit them soon.

'Now can we talk about how school and yourself would like to communicate from now on?'

Jane is considerably calmer by now, although very far from being smiley and relaxed.

'All I've ever had from you is trouble,' she says, looking at Helen.

'Jane, I think you may mean school in general, don't you, as Helen has only been here a short while?'

'What would you like me to do Jane?' Helen smiles at her.

'I think,' says George, 'Jane would like to feel she is working with you, rather than against you, isn't that right, Jane?'

'Aye, I would. I need to know what's happening day to

day, because she's not going to tell me anything good. We ought to be aware of what's going on both at school and at home.'

'How about a home/school diary? And maybe we could meet, or at least I could phone you every week with an update?' Helen is generously adding to her already considerable workload.

'Is there any more training needed?' asks George. Helen agrees to investigate how staff could be brought up to date on PDA and Tourette's.

'And maybe something about wrestling, perhaps?' George adds mischievously. There is a ripple of laughter round the table.

'It's not on the curriculum, but I will ask.' Says Helen. 'Could liven up our PE lessons a bit.'

'That would do wonders for Zoe's self-esteem, I think!' George grins.

'Poor Zoe,' he thinks, looking at the angry face of her mother. 'I wonder if wrestling is the only meaningful form of human physical contact she has in her life.'

He brings the proceedings to a close amid smiles and thanks, and leaves them all chatting amiably round the table.

After the long drive home, he writes up the case, sends off the agreement to all the parties, and thinks about what to cook for his tea. He takes another look at the questionnaire that Zoe filled in.

'What are the main things you would like to change?'

'Being listened to and not getting shouted at when I'm talking.

Not being upset all the time.
Not feeling poorly all the time.
Teacher being nice to me.
Children getting told off when being mean to me.'

Just as he is signing off on his computer, there is an email from the mother.

'I get home today to find Zoe has just been excluded for swearing. What should I do?'

Zoe's revenge

Yeeeeaaaayy! No more school for two days! No-school heaven! No more bloody teachers. No more bloody kids to annoy me. No more bloody work. Well, they gave me some stuff to do but I'm not gonna do it. Why should I? Work is for school, not home. Home is not school. Home is like, home, innit? No-one can make me do anything at home, least of all my stupid mother. Stupid mother she always wanting me to do stuff, like, tidy your room, clear up the dishes, take dog for a walk, help little brother with his buttons, he'll learn soon enough not to go around with his pants undone.

And always them telling me, no swearing Zoe, no swearing, no fucking swearing. I wasn't swearing was I! I don't swear, do I! At least not on purpose. Do I swear on purpose? Course I bloody don't. 's not as if other kids don't swear, do they. Bloody teachers don't hear them always swearing out there. Why don't they hear them swearing out there? I hear them swearing. They hear me swearing. They don't get in trouble for it. Why's it always me I wanna know. Why me? They don't like me do they!

That man at the hospital he didn't mind did he. He didn't say I shouldn't swear. And if he says it's all right then It's all right. Why is it all right in some places and not in others. Eh? All right in the playground, not all right in the class, not all right at home, cos me little brother might pick it up. Well, he's already picked it up int'e! Only she don't know do she. Or she don't think he does it. But I know he does all right, little sod. I know he does.

So, me mum says they were havin' a meeting about me swearing and a lot of other stuff and not doing any work and annoying other kids, and then annoying me. And she says this man called a mediator were there to sort it all out, and I dunno what one o' them is, but she says he sorted it all out and everyone's gonna be nice to me from now on if I can be nice to them. And while all that's going on there, they are in the class telling me not to come back tomorrow because of swearing! Me mum was mad when she got home.

God, what I have to put up with from her! They don't know what I have to put up with. Always on at me for something. I'm the eldest, she says, so I have to set an example. Well, I don't feel like the eldest, do I. She's the eldest anyway. I wanna be the youngest, then I might get some sympathy. How can I be the eldest when I'm, like, only ten. What does it mean – set an example? Wish she would tell me what I'm supposed to do. All she does is tell me what I'm NOT supposed to do. All the things I like doing I'm Not supposed to do.

She don't get it. When she tells me to do something, tells me, mind, not ask me, then my head says, Don't do it Zoe, don't do it. And even if she ever asked me, which she never does, I still don't wanna do it, do I. If she ever asked me to do something I might actually want to do, which she never does, then I might, like, actually do it. But she don't. She just keeps on telling me to do things, then she tells me off for not doing it. She can't seem to get that! Why can't she get it? She must be stupid. Stupid cow. If it came up and hit her on the nose she still wouldn't get it. They don't know how stupid she is at that school. All she does is complain about them, to me, and complain about me to them. Duh!!

As for him… little brother… god, who'd have a little brother? What are little brothers for? Eh? What use are they? All he ever does is bloody cry. And then I get the blame, don't I. I'm supposed to kick a ball around for him, and then if it hits him on the nose he cries, or if it goes over the fence he cries, what am I supposed to do with a ball? That's what dads are for innit. And what happened to him then? Where is the dad in this story? She says he left because of me, something else she can blame me for. Fucking useless dad he was, if he can't look after his own kids. So little brother cries and cries 'cos he aint got no dad, I don't get that. Lots o' kids don't have a dad, and they're not crying all the time.

So little brother gets away with murder. Like when he wet his pants, she comes Oh little love, never mind, let's take 'em off and get you cleaned up then. So, he cries some more and then he gets a cuddle. Bet she wouldn't do that if I pissed me knickers. And if he won't eat his dinner, she's like, what's a matter love, don't you like that? Come on let's have a try, and she sits with him spooning it down his gob like a baby. Like he's fucking four years old, inne. Makes me wanna spit. And if I don't eat the stuff she's just burnt, I get it in the neck. She'd make the fucking Pope swear, she would.

So, I get two days off. Them two bloody women what are supposed to teach me in that little room half the time, they don't get it do they! Sitting in there with six other kids who can barely read and write or even speak, how am I supposed to learn anything, if we're like, going at a snail's pace all day, and they can hardly string two words together. Booooooring! And they're so bloody patient with 'em. How can they be so patient with them stupid bozo's and not with me? And I'm doing stuff from another lesson to them, so they are trying to juggle us all at the same time, and I might as well be on me own, I'd get on a lot faster, and a lot quieter.

And that light on the ceiling, can't they hear the buzzing noise that makes. Why can't they hear it? Do I have different sort of ears to everyone else? I can't concentrate with that buzzing. So, I get annoyed what with the noise of the bozo's struggling to speak and understand simple stuff and all that buzzing, so if I start to say something they say I'm swearing. When I just wanna ask a question or just wanna get out. So that's one way to get two days off. What a relief!

And there's play times. Big noise times. Big boys make noise times. Balls flying all over, boys chasing balls, scoring goals, shouting out and hugging each other like them stupid men on tv. I just wanna curl up in a corner to get away from the noise. But there aren't any corners in our playground where you can, like, chill out on your own, because we have to be watched all the time. And girls huddling together with their mobiles like robots, they are allowed to do that at play times, god knows why they have to keep looking at their bloody phones, even talking to each other on them, as if they weren't already there. So, teachers have to take them off them again when they go back in. Stupid.

There's just me and Sophie, my sometimes friend. We walk round the edges together trying not to get hit by flying balls. She don't like noise either, but she don't swear, and get told off like me, so I hardly ever see her except at play times, cos she's in class and I'm not. And anyway, we sometimes fall out, because she don't wanna do what I wanna do, and after I hit her a few times we got separated, didn't we, so I'm left with no friends. Except she wanders back to find me now and then and we moan about teachers and other kids. And, wonder of wonders, my mum lets her come to my house once or twice, and we watch tv in my room, without little brother, like HEAVEN!

So. They're talking about high school. Next September. If I can stick it out here till then that is. Or if they can stick me much longer. I see them going up the road to that bloody awful school in them ridiculous uniforms. Wearing a tie would you believe, what they cut in half so it only takes up half the space on their chest. And the girls hitching up their skirts so they look like Beyonce or Taylor Swift. And the boys guzzling sugary drinks in cans what they throw over our garden wall when they're empty. Bloody boys. Bloody hell!

Me and Sophie we talked about it. She don't wanna go either. But we all gotta go somewhere. Not that I'd wanna stay at this hell hole much longer. Having to put up with the same teachers all day every day. And them bozo's, would they be allowed to go there? Do all schools have bozo's? Would I be with the bozo class again? Are there any special schools for bozo's? What about special schools for girls who swear and whistle and refuse to do any work? Mum said we gotta go and look at some soon, and I better be on my best behaviour or they won't take me. Chance would be a fine thing. Can I see myself going to high school? Yeah, why not? Can't be much worse than here. I could be thrown out of five lessons a day. Mum thinks they have a special quiet area for kids who can't cope. I wonder if they do wrestling?

Wrestling. Wrestling! I love it! My one time of the week. My special time. The only time I know what to do. When I am in charge. No bozo's. No 'teaching assistants'. No books. No teachers. Lots of space. Lots of physical. Like, I can let it all out. Like, I don't need to swear. I can swear with my body, especially when it hurts. I love chucking people around. I love being chucked around. Yeah. Like not with words or telling off, but hands and legs and action. That's me!

When big sisters come round to our house (from dad's first marriage) that's what we do. We have a bit of a laugh. We don't say nice things like how are you, what have you been up to. We just grab hold of each other and wrestle each other up the stairs and round the garden. Think they're a bit like me. Must run in his family. Wrestling and swearing. They understand.

That's what I can do. When we go to these other schools I can ask – do you do wrestling? And if they say no, I can say why not? If I can do wrestling every day then I might do some work for you. You let me do wrestling then I might agree to come here.

All them bleedin' psychos, paedos, psych-what-evers who come and see me, if they could just let me show them a bit of wrestling in their posh little offices, if I could just say come outside and wrestle with me for a few minutes, and then you can write your bloody reports. And put in it, Zoe likes to wrestle. Zoe is a wrestler. That's what Zoe needs. All right?

PEOPLE PIE: JUICY PORTRAITS IN POETRY
Available in paperback and as an ebook

Paperback ISBN: 978-1-915494-12-2
eBook ISBN: 978-1-839785-50-4